the nation within

pantheon books, a division of random house, new york

Francis
Fytton

the
nation
within

for Anne Richards
who came to the rescue when I was wounded by the *flics*

L'Armée est une nation dans la nation; c'est un vice de nos temps.
—Alfred de Vigny, *sur le caractère général des armées, Servitude et grandeur militaires*

manifestation

⊕ He came breathless up the steps of the Metro and into the place Saint-Michel. The rain bent his bare head: the up-turned collar of his trenchcoat blinkered him. Still running, he turned left and crossed the rue de la Huchette in two strides, curbstone to curbstone; then slipped and sprawled, so that he lay gasping like a freshly landed fish.

"*Merde*," he said with the last of his breath.

As he spoke the man saw that he was lying among the debris of a disaster.

He was surrounded by shoes.

The shoes had been so recently discarded that some still reeked of their owners' feet. They represented both sexes: several classes, and all ages. There were the tooled leather mules of the Mussulman housewife; shoes with square toes and stiletto heels, representing the fashionable Parisienne; the pointed two-tones of the prowling *boulevardier*; black boots, with crushed toes and trailing laces, of laboring men; and the shoes of children. There was a baby's shoe beside his right hand: he picked it up.

It was then that he saw the blood upon his right hand. He retched and repressed the vomit.

But there was no cut upon his hand.

He was lying on the brink of a great pool of blood: it covered one curbstone: the rain was making oily splashes on the surface; but it did little to dilute the blood; the blood was thicker than the water.

And then he saw that there was blood upon his cuff, just below the gilt buckles, and he scrambled to his feet. His fumbling left hand extracted a handkerchief from his breast pocket and carefully wiped the cuff clean. Then he screwed the handkerchief into a sodden ball and stuffed it into his pocket.

"What a mess," he said aloud. "It must have been a traffic accident. I hope the police got the driver."

Then he saw the police. The blue ranks were drawn up across the pont Saint-Michel, whose lamps silhouetted them against the massy bulk beneath the flèche spire of the Palais de Justice on the Ile de la Cité. They were dangling batons or nursing submachine guns.

There was a fire engine at the corner of the quai Saint-Michel and another, facing it, in the mouth of the quai des Grands-Augustins. Their hoses were coupled to the mains and the crews had leveled the nozzles at pedestrian height. Then an officer of the Régiment des Sapeurs et Pompiers came into the *place* with uplifted hand.

"Come along, my children. Let's leave this sort of thing to the *flics*. It's all they're fit for. They're out for blood. They don't need our water."

As the firemen ran to disconnect the hoses and the great engines reverberated with life, a major of police, steel-rimmed spectacles glinting beneath a silver-braided kepi, ran up: he was shouting his anger.

The fire officer strode past him, leather jacket sodden with rain, but stiff with the pride of his profession.

"There has been a manifestation," the man told himself. "A manifestation."

The fire engines thundered away and now he was alone in the sodden *place* save for the police. He had been running toward the file. He hesitated, then went on at a walk. He was going toward the Café de la Gare, on the corner of the *place* and the quai Saint-Michel. Only now he kept his eyes upon the barred bridge as he walked.

Broken glass crackled beneath the thin soles of now sodden suede shoes, and he had to step over the remains of a motor scooter that had been broken as a child's tin toy is broken. The glass windows of the Café de la Gare were shattered; broken slivers of glass leaned out of their frames: they shone like spearheads in the rain. The interior gleamed blue-bright beneath a wealth of fluorescent lights, but it appeared to be deserted.

The man tried the still intact door, but it was locked. He rapped on the glass. Then he saw something moving above the level of the zinc-topped counter. It was a pink and highly polished dome: it was like a captive balloon moving in a light breeze.

Then the man saw that the dome was encircled by a fringe of grey hair: it emerged as the head of the waiter.

The man rapped again upon the glass door and pointed toward the pont Saint-Michel.

"Napoléon," the man called.

The waiter now rose to reveal himself of a similar stature to his namesake: thick eyebrows appeared to crawl up to the polished dome of his skull as he recognized the visitor. He began to move along the counter toward the door.

"Let me in, Napoléon," the man shouted. "I need an armagnac."

"I'm coming, monsieur," the waiter said in the guttural accent of Corsica.

Then other heads began to appear above the counter; they were followed by hands that laid hold of the waiter known as Napoléon: hands formed into fists and were shaken at the man who stood at the door, then unclenched as fingertips were flicked in dismissal.

He turned away then. He did not turn his back upon the police, however, but his flank as he moved back toward the Metro, stumbling over shoes and splinters of glass, slipping in pools of blood, until he reached the steps and descended into the warm wave of urine-perfumed air. He hesitated before the ticket office and then, stiffening his well-padded shoulders, continued along the passage until he came to the exit in the place Saint-André-des-Arts.

At this point he was out of sight of the police. The *place* contained four cafés with elaborate awnings surmounted by apartments that seemed to stagger with Mediterranean abandon after the geometric severity of Haussmann; and three of the cafés were closed. So the man approached the Café-Tabac Saint-André-des-Arts. It was crowded with people drinking at the bar or playing the pinball machines, but the man found the doors locked.

He rapped sharply on the glass and a stout barman with a head like a Charolais bull came at once to open it.

"What are you doing, Monsieur Hanna?" he asked. He made the name sound like "Anna."

"Let me in, Gaston," said the man called Hanna. "You know I have nothing to do with this nonsense."

"All right, but get a move on or I'll be in trouble."

But as he opened the door wider, the manager came running: a little man in a grey cardigan whose soiled left sleeve had been stained by his snotting nose.

"You can't come in here," he shouted. "You're an Algerian Mussulman. What do you think would happen to my café if the police found you here?"

The manager was addressing him as "thou" instead of "you."

"Monsieur Hanna is from the Lebanon," the stout waiter said stoutly.

"He is a Mussulman."

"No, I am a Christian and I have applied for French citizenship," Hanna said.

"So much the worse for you," said the manager: he slammed and locked the door.

"Listen, you Fascist prick," Hanna shouted, "I am more of a Frenchman than you are."

The manager opened the door to shout back, "Tell that to the *flics*." Then he slammed the door again.

Hanna turned away: he walked blindly across the *place* and stopped before the fountain on the corner of the Boul' Mich' and the place Saint-André-des-Arts. He looked up at the figure of Saint Michael overthrowing Satan: Saint Michael was grinding his heel into Satan's neck and the devil was looking thoroughly downcast. A plaque informed him that it had been erected at the meeting place of the fifth and sixth *arrondissements* in honor of the inhabitants who had risen against the Nazi garrison from August 18 to 25, 1944, and of the dead.

"I am a Frenchman," he said aloud, looking up at the figures. He struck himself on the chest, but not very hard. "I am a better Frenchman than those pricks."

"If you are a Frenchman, Georges Hanna, you had better join the French," someone answered him. The surname had become harsh: "Hgan-nah."

Hanna started: the speaker had been a woman; she had spoken Arabic.

Hanna looked down to earth and saw several figures beyond the low iron railings in the shadow of the fountain. They were seated on the lip of the basin into which the fountain fell and dabbling in the water, as worshippers might perform a rite. But as his sight penetrated the shadows, Hanna saw that they were dipping their handkerchiefs in the water and bathing the blood off one another's faces.

The girl was graceful, with gamin-frizzy hair; she had exaggeratedly Semitic features; the skin about her eyes was so dark and deep that it seemed bruised; the eyes themselves seemed to gleam: African eyes: the eyes of a lioness.

"So it's you, Nefissa Saddok," Hanna said. "I might have known you were mixed up in this nonsense. You can't taunt me. My culture is French: it is my language."

"But you were born an Arab in the Lebanon," she said.

"Of blood mixed with God knows how many races, and I have applied for naturalization."

The girl turned back to bathing the face of a Mussulman woman with a baby in her arms. The woman wore traditional robes of green and white: the colors of the Algerian National Liberation Front, the FLN. She had a tattoo mark between the eyes. Just above that a fresh wound cut a lightning path into the hairline. Blood was running down the woman's nose: Nefissa was trying to stanch it, but the woman was impatient. The baby was crying on a high, constant note, only just audi-

ble above the falling water. The woman was pointing to one
of its feet, which lacked a shoe.

"What will my baby do without his shoe?" she asked
Nefissa. "He will catch cold and my husband cannot afford to
buy him another pair, now that he is out of work."

"Where is your husband?" Nefissa asked.

"I think the police took him away. He is a man: he can
look after himself. But what will my poor baby do without his
shoe?"

Hanna found that he had been clutching the baby's shoe
ever since his fall: he stepped over the railing and tried it on
the infant's foot: it fitted perfectly: it matched the other shoe.
The baby stopped crying: he began to coo contentedly, kicking his newly shod feet in the air.

"Thank you, monsieur, thank you," the woman said. She
seized and kissed Hanna's hand. Blood trickled down her
forehead and splashed his sleeve in the place that he had just
wiped clean. The woman stood up, brushing Nefissa aside,
and shuffled away.

"That was good of you, Georges," Nefissa said. "I always
knew you were a good man—really a good man."

"What gave you that idea?"

"You cannot bear to see people hurt."

"It was nothing," he said.

"Only your saying it was nothing can make nothing of it,"
she said.

Hanna did not reply and Nefissa looked at him for a long
time. Then she held both hands palm downward at waist level
and suddenly raised them upward and outward so that they
faced him, palm upward, at shoulder height: it was as though
she were despairing of him. When the gesture was completed,
she turned away and went to two other green-and-white-robed
women who were bathing the bloodied head of an old man.
The old man was saying, "What a thing! What a thing! To be
wounded by the police at my age. I'm seventy-four. Would
you believe that? What a thing to be wounded at my age. I'm

seventy-four. Would you believe that? Would you think the *flics* would bother with a man of my age? They know I'm still dangerous. That's it. Gently now, gently. That hurts. I'm not as young as I used to be. I'm seventy-four."

"What happened?" asked Hanna.

The two women looked at him and then looked away. Nefissa had found another handkerchief and was bathing the old man's head above the left ear: dark blood was oozing out of a wound and trickling down inside his collar. Nefissa did not turn.

"What happened?" Hanna repeated. "Will someone please tell me what happened?"

The old man suddenly inserted a blunt forefinger in his ear, gouged out a quantity of blood, and shook his head vigorously.

"The police hit us," the old man said. "That's what happened. The police hit us. They even hit a poor old man like me. They know I'm still dangerous. I'm seventy-four. Would you believe the *flics* would hit a man of seventy-four?"

"But why did the police hit you?" Hanna asked.

"You should know," Nefissa said suddenly. "You Frenchman."

"Listen," said Hanna. "Listen to me. I have spent the past month with my family in Beirut. I only returned this afternoon. I came here to walk along the Boul' Mich' and see how the Left Bank was looking. I'd be there now, but I decided to shelter in the Café de la Gare until the rain stopped. How could I know what was happening?"

"You were looking for a girl?" Nefissa said.

"Yes," replied Hanna, "I was looking for a French girl who, even though she did not shave her pubic hair and perform hygienic intimacies with her left hand, would not abstain from sex until her marriage, which is the convention among women of your race and religion." Only he said this without speaking.

So he said aloud, "I was going to have a glass of armagnac.

Perhaps two glasses of armagnac." He was sweating: the palms of his hands itched and the insides of his thighs were sweat-clammy.

"Alcohol," she said.

"I am a Christian," he reminded her.

"Nevertheless you are an Arab."

"I come from Mount Lebanon," he said. "You would not understand. For a century we Maronites have enjoyed French protection from the Druses."

"How very selective the French are," Nefissa said. She said this in French with an exaggeratedly shrill Parisian accent. "For the past century they have been persecuting us Algerian Mussulmans. *Ooh, là. Zut, alors. Merde. Va-t'en faire foutre.*"

"Listen," Hanna said. "You should keep out of politics. You really should. You're too young, too pretty. A girl like you should keep out of politics." He was shaking all over. He began to say, "You should keep me out of politics," but the words would not come off his lips for the trembling.

"It is not politics this time," Nefissa said. "It is economics."

"What is economics?" Hanna asked.

When Hanna said this, he began to tremble again. His left knee began to shake violently: he drew his shoulders up to his ears.

"What is economics?" Hanna repeated.

"What happened tonight," Nefissa said.

"Listen," said Hanna. "This is none of my business. I am an Arab by blood, but a Frenchman by culture. I spend nine hours a day at the desk of a French airline. I learned to speak French before I could speak Arabic."

"When did you learn to speak Arabic?" asked Nefissa.

"You cannot insult me by saying that," Hanna said.

"I cannot insult you," Nefissa said.

They were now speaking in French.

"What happened tonight?" Hanna asked. The shaking had ceased. He drew a pack of Celtiques out of the pocket of his trenchcoat. He pulled the red band and peeled the cellophane off the top. He inserted the nail of his right forefinger beneath the fold of the silver paper and tore off a triangle at the corner. He tapped up two cigarettes by flicking the bottom of the pack with his middle finger. He offered the pack to Nefissa. She struck it aside and he withdrew it to avoid a spill: Celtiques cost NF 1.65 a pack. He took a cigarette between his lips from the pack and lighted it. He flicked the spent match into the fountain.

"All right," he said. "What happened tonight?" He had ceased to tremble.

"There was a manifestation," she said.

"I guessed that."

"Do you know who these people are?"

Hanna looked around, but they were now quite alone by the fountain: the old man and the women were gone.

"They are Algerians," he said. "They are Mussulmans."

"They are waiters and café proprietors with their wives and children," she said. "Does that mean nothing to you?"

"No."

"They were protesting because the Prefect of Police in Paris, Maurice Papon, has ordered all Mussulman-owned cafés to be closed by seven thirty and all Mussulmans to be off the streets by midnight. In fact, he has even advised them for their own good not to go out after sunset. That means the cafés have no trade, so the waiters are fired and the proprietors are almost bankrupt. And do you know what happens then? The Minister of the Interior, Roger Frey, has ordered that all Mussulmans who are out of work shall be deported to Algeria."

"I read about that," Hanna said. "It was a move against the FLN. After all, sixteen *flics* have already been assassinated this year and more than forty wounded."

"And how many Algerians have been assassinated by the *flics*?"

"I don't know."

"You don't know because you didn't read the figures. Figures of that sort aren't published."

"Anyway, they're only being sent back to their own country. I can't see that that's any great hardship."

"You can't see very much except what you read in *Le Figaro*, can you? Algeria is not their country: they are Frenchmen who happen to be Mussulmans. Many of them cannot even speak Arabic. Their homes and their families are in France. They have nothing to return to. They will be put behind barbed wire to starve. There is no work in Algeria because of the war."

"Well, you can't accuse the French of starting the war," Hanna said. "You're like all professional intellectuals: when the burden of intellectual life becomes too heavy for you, you substitute emotion for reason. The FLN began this war. They even made war on their own people, the Algerian National Movement, because the MNA wanted autonomy by peaceful means. If the Algerian people are suffering so much they'd better join the French in getting rid of the FLN. They wouldn't last long unless they were sheltered and financed by the majority of Mussulmans."

"Perhaps they don't want to get rid of the FLN."

"Then the FLN should stop the war if it doesn't want the Algerian people to suffer. They can't have it both ways. Why doesn't the FLN stop the war?"

Nefissa stood up so suddenly that Hanna recoiled: but she only seized him by the forearms.

"Listen," she said. "You were right when you said I had abandoned reason for emotion. But you don't know why I did so. Will you let me show you? Tonight the Mussulman columns are leaving the slums and the shantytowns to march on central Paris. To show that their intentions are peaceful, each column is accompanied by women and children. They are putting their trust in the *flics*. You, who wish to become a Frenchman, can do no less. Come with me and see how the war is being fought and then perhaps you will understand why it is being fought."

"Yes," Hanna said. He seemed so surprised at hearing the word on his lips that he repeated it. "Yes," he said. He had begun to tremble again: he was tensing his stomach and sphincter muscles against the urge to defecate. He covered the girl's hand with his own and their fingers interlaced like those of lovers. Her hand was warm and firm and she increased the pressure of her fingers until his own trembling ceased. "Let's go," Hanna said. "Let's march with the column." The trembling had ceased. "Let's go," he repeated.

"Good," Nefissa said: she lifted her head as though to toss her hair back, but it was too short to toss. She unclasped her fingers, but slipped her hand through Hanna's arm. "Let's go there," she said.

So they stepped over the railings and were back in the place Saint-Michel. As they did so a group of Algerians came from the rue Saint-Séverin. And Hanna began to tremble again as they crossed the road to join them.

The demonstrators were at once fierce and feeble: some of the men had fearful head wounds: one youth had a gash from cheekbone to chin through which could be seen the bloodied teeth; the scalp of a man was split like the skin of an orange; the ear of another was hanging by a thread of gristle; and a man in dungarees paused to spit teeth into the gutter.

They began to mill about aimlessly and exclaim at the sight of one another's wounds. After a time they moved along the pavement. There were many French people strolling in the upper reaches of the Boul' Mich': they gave the Mussulmans right of way and then stopped to stare after them.

Nefissa drew Hanna into the thick of the marching Mussulmans.

As the demonstrators reached the crossroads formed by the boulevard Saint-Germain and the Boul' Mich' a cloudburst halted them. It was more like an explosion of water than a downpour. So sudden and heavy was the rain that they were all soaked before they could take cover. Nefissa and Hanna joined the majority in sheltering beneath the awnings of a corner shoe shop. Some of the demonstrators ran out into the rain with their handkerchiefs outspread; when these were saturated they went back under cover to bathe the heads of the wounded.

"Why don't the wounded stand out in the rain until the rain washes their heads clean?" Hanna asked.

Now Nefissa was trembling. Hanna looked at her with his mouth hanging open. He clasped her thin, chill hand where it clutched his left forearm. She was trembling from the tips of her fingers.

"This is what the French have done to us," she told him. "Just see for yourself what the French have done."

"Did they attack the police?"

"It happened as I said."

"You didn't tell me how it happened," he said. "Only why it happened."

"You'll see how it happened," she said. "If you stay with us."

"Come and have an armagnac," Hanna said. "It will warm you up."

"You forget that I am a Mussulman and alcohol is forbidden to us."

"I've seen you drinking alcohol before," he said. "Most Mussulmans seem to drink wine or beer in France."

"That is because the French are trying to pervert us," Nefissa said. "We must learn to fight their temptations."

"Have a coffee anyway. It will do you good."

"No café will serve us tonight. They won't have Mussulmans on their premises."

"Come to my room then," Hanna urged. "I can make you a cup of coffee. I only live in the rue Mouffetard. We can have a cup of coffee and you can tell me what happened in the manifestation. That will do more good than trailing around in the rain. The manifestation is over. It's too wet to do anything more."

"Look," Nefissa said. "Here come reinforcements. The manifestation will go on."

Two more groups of Mussulmans were running toward them: one came down the Boul' Mich', forcing its way through the traffic at the crossroads; the other came from the eastern end of the boulevard Saint-Germain, from the direc-

tion of the Mussulman quarter of the medieval district known
as Saint-Julien-le-Pauvre. This second group, Hanna learned
from Nefissa's inquiries, had been separated from the original
column in the clash with the police: some had scalp wounds
washed clean by rain. But the group from the Boul' Mich' had
not yet been involved in fighting: they were fresh and vigor-
ous: many were students.

These newcomers put new life into the bloody remnant of
the column that Nefissa and Hanna had joined. There were
cries of "*Allah akhbah!*" as they met.

"God is greatest," Hanna said. "But that doesn't make us
greater than the police." Then he corrected himself. "Not us,
them."

"This is no time for an infidel to blaspheme," Nefissa said.
"You will see who is greatest. Let's go there." She had
stopped shivering.

The rain was still falling but it was forgotten. A number of
serious young men in blue or brown trenchcoats had come
with the Boul' Mich' group: they affected the survivors of the
clash like a blood transfusion. The trenchcoated young men
began to clap: then everyone was clapping. One-two-three,
pause, one-two-three.

"I thought you said this was a nonpolitical manifestation,"
Hanna said to Nefissa.

"So it is."

"But they're clapping to the time of the FLN slogan: *Al-gé-
rie, al-gé-rienne.*"

"That's right," said one of the trenchcoated young men in
passing. "Why aren't you clapping?"

Hanna began to clap.

At a signal from the trenchcoated leaders, the demonstrators surged across the Boul' Mich'. The street was almost solid
with traffic going south from central Paris: the police must
have lifted their barricades across the pont Saint-Michel, to
release the pent-up traffic. A traffic policeman in a streaming
white raincoat decided to go off duty when he saw the Mussulmans come clapping across the street. He made a way for

himself through the traffic by rapping the slowly moving cars with his white baton.

The Mussulmans began to laugh. Some of them began to imitate the policeman in his fear and in his authority: they rapped on the hoods and doors of the cars. Some of the motorists responded by blowing their horns, which was illegal, but the Mussulmans only rapped harder and crowded the cars to a standstill. The horn-blowing ceased and there were white faces at the windshields.

Thus the mob won a passage for itself and became a column again when it reached the western side of the Boul' Mich' and defiled into the boulevard Saint-Germain. They were now perhaps three hundred strong and gaining strength at every step as stragglers rejoined the marching ranks. Some of the newcomers carried shoes. They ran along the column asking those who limped in bare or stockinged feet if the shoes would fit them. The young men in trenchcoats kept jumping on seats and urging the marchers to form orderly files and keep out of the roadway where they would impede oncoming traffic. The column was becoming more orderly. At each crossing the young men appointed themselves traffic wardens: they held up the column until the lights changed to green, or if there were no lights, signaled the cars to wait.

"Where are we going?" Hanna asked one of the trench-coated young men.

"To meet our destiny."

"No doubt," Hanna said, "but I presume we have a physical destination as well as a spiritual destiny."

"We are coming to the cafés of Saint-Germain-des-Prés," the young man said. "The intellectuals will be there. French intellectuals, you understand. They will join us and their presence will deter the police."

"That's all very well if the intellectuals support you and the police permit you to get through," Hanna said.

"Aren't you a French intellectual?" the young man asked.

"Me? Oh, yes, of course," Hanna said.

"Then no doubt you can encourage your friends to join us."

"I'll try."

The young man leaped onto a seat in between two drunken bums and began clapping his hands over his head. Then he led the chant *"Al-gé-rie, al-gé-rienne."* It was taken up by the column. And in this way they approached the cafés of the carrefour Saint-Germain-des-Prés.

At the Old Navy very young faces gaped at them through the insulating glass terrace; from the congested apron of the Rhumerie Martinique bearded faces and shaggy heads stared over their heads; outside the Deux Magots consciously refined faces were engaged in sudden conversations; and within the Café de Flore painted male faces ogled them. The clapping ceased, the chant died away.

Only one young Frenchman tried to join the column. He wore a workman's leather jacket. He staggered and tried to fall in step with the column, but there was no step. One of the trenchcoated young men spoke to him.

"You don't want to be picked up by the *flics* when you are pissed as a Pole, do you now? Keep out of trouble."

And the young workman staggered off across the boulevard, picking a drunkard's lucky path through the traffic.

Despite the self-appointed traffic wardens, a taxi driver tried to force his Peugeot 403 through the ranks as they debouched beneath the Norman tower of Saint-Germain. A young Mussulman with a bloodied forehead struck the windshield and shouted. The driver tried to press on. The Mussulman began to wrench open the driver's door. Then two of the self-appointed wardens, expostulating, took him by the arms and made a way for the taxi through the column.

"Do you know where we're going now?" Hanna asked Nefissa. They were still marching westward along the boulevard Saint-Germain. Then he changed it to "Where are they going?"

"Let's go and ask them," Nefissa suggested.

She took him by the arm and led him to the head of the column; she was tugging because Hanna was dragging his feet.

The column was led by two men. One was about twenty-five: his face was only bone structure; his hair was cropped to a shadow so that he had the appearance of great resolution. He wore a glossy blue trenchcoat with gilt buckles: it was an even better garment than that which Hanna wore. He was walking just outside the line of parked cars; his jaw muscles were flexing continually; and when he turned to exhort the column, silhouetted against the street lights, it was like a face from the Grand Guignol. And yet he only urged his followers to keep order. He was speaking in French. While doing this he collided with a Frenchman who, coming in the opposite direction, had stepped off the pavement to give the marchers the right of way. The Frenchman recoiled, as though expecting a blow. The leader at once put his arm around the man's shoulders and said, "I'm sorry. We are for peace. We mean you no harm."

"The Reaper himself is leading us," Hanna said.

The man who walked behind the leader could have been a Frenchman: he had brown wavy hair and fair skin. He wore a sheepskin jacket, a silk scarf knotted at the back, and fashionably tight trousers. But he spoke Arabic.

"*Imshi, imshi,*" he was urging them. "Get a move on, get a move on."

"Now, where are we going?" Hanna asked.

"They will tell us," Nefissa said.

"What do you want to know?" the deputy leader asked.

"Where you are leading us," Nefissa said. "My friend wants to know."

"Ask him," the deputy said, pointing to the leader.

The leader smiled at Nefissa: his teeth were big and white and even: when he smiled his head was more than ever like a skull. "I know you," he told Nefissa. "You are a militant. You want to know where we are going? We are marching to the Chamber of Deputies. We could not find justice before the

Palais de Justice, but we will speak before the Parliament. The deputies will hear us and see our wounds."

"We are with you," Nefissa said.

"Are you a Frenchman?" he asked Hanna.

"I hope to be one day," Hanna said.

"He is from the Lebanon," Nefissa explained.

"What are you doing here?" asked the leader.

"I want to learn the truth," Hanna said in Arabic.

"You will learn the truth," the leader replied in French. "It will be an education."

As he spoke a police Dauphine painted black and white drove slowly past the column from head to tail, the light on the roof throwing an intermittent amber glow on their faces as it revolved. There was a *flic* in a silver-braided kepi sitting beside the driver and speaking into a microphone: it was the major Hanna had seen in the place Saint-Michel.

The leader of the column put his arms about the shoulders of Nefissa and Hanna.

"Listen, my children," he said. "Please walk in the second file if you are going to remain with us. I am sure the police are going to charge us again: the shock will be terrible. It is for us to bear."

"We will bear it with you," Nefissa said, but Hanna dragged on her arm and now the other trenchcoated young men thrust ahead to form the first file.

They were now almost opposite the Palladian façade of the Ministry of War. Hanna was on the outside of the second file: he saw first the long line of *paniers-salades* drawn up at the opposite curb: the black containers of the law. Then he saw the security forces: they were in three sections: he had never before seen so many police.

The vanguard was a Republican Security Company in coal-scuttle helmets and blue battle dress: they carried the yard-long, lead-tipped truncheons or Sten guns; second were the Gendarmerie nationale, theatrical in their leather gaiters and blue trousers with fancy piping, glistening black waterproofs, and poilu helmets of the First World War, formidable with their carbines and wooden-stocked MAS 54 submachine guns; and lastly an intervention force of the Municipal Police, their blue capes sodden and sagging with the weight of lead sewn into the linings; they also carried truncheons.

The Algerian column halted, so that it straddled the mouth of the rue de Bellechasse.

Beneath the sodium lamps, dark faces turned sickly and began to sweat. The letters "CRS" were passed along from mouth to mouth down the Mussulman files; no one noticed the Gendarmerie nationale, nor the intervention police.

But the two groups were still separated by the swift stream of traffic, which was two-way in this section of the boulevard. So that they stood, watching one another, alert but insulated, over the roofs of the cars.

Then the skull-faced leader cried, *"Avancez!"* and the cry was taken up by his lieutenants.

No one moved.

"Why are they speaking French now?" Hanna asked Nefissa, holding her tightly so that she could not advance.

"Many of them understand only French," she said. "They have spent their lives in France. They speak no Arabic. They are French men and women, but of the wrong race and religion."

The word *"Avancez"* was still being thrown by the leaders as a counter to the initials "CRS" in the ranks; and suddenly a group of women in the fifth and sixth files, some of them carrying babies, began to move forward; and the whole column advanced.

With the same suddenness the traffic ceased: the *flics* must have halted it before and behind the column. As the last car sped away, the CRS broke ranks and charged. They were followed by the gendarmes and the police. They came uttering grunts and cries. The only distinguishable words were *"On les aura."*

The Mussulman column at once broke and ran. The leader and his lieutenants fanned out as they ran, like sheepdogs screening their sheep from a wolf pack. The bulk of the column retreated back up the boulevard Saint-Germain, taking the women with them. But those foremost, caught between the charge in front and the press behind, plunged into the side street, carrying Nefissa and Hanna like corks on an ebb tide. They were jamming and jostling one another between a double line of cars parked bumper to bumper in the rue de Bellechasse.

Hanna seized Nefissa and used the point of his right shoulder to draw her clear of the rout and into a doorway. It was rather shallow: they flattened their buttocks against the iron-studded woodwork and waited.

And then the slaughter began.

The CRS, being less heavily accoutered, were first into the street. The leading man overtook an elderly Mussulman on the pavement, struck him on the back of the head with his truncheon, turned his wrist to give him a back-handed blow in the face, and ran on. The old man turned, his face masked by blood, and fell. A gendarme came in pursuit of the trench-coated young men. He drove the steel-shod butt of his MAS 54 into the nape of the fugitive's neck and then into the kidneys. The young man fell forward on his face, began to scream, then rolled on his back, legs flailing. The gendarme raised the submachine gun high above his head and drove the butt into his face, so that the bones crackled as they broke. Then he kicked the Mussulman in the head with either foot and ran on making noises that resounded like snarls. Another CRS man pinned a Mussulman against the opposite wall and hit him in the crotch with the butt of his Sten. As the Mussulman went down the CRS man struck him across the face with the gun barrel. Then he drove the butt two or three times into the Mussulman's face and kicked him in the stomach. The Mussulman rolled over and the CRS man began to flail his back with gun and feet.

The street was full of hunting police. They caught Mussulmans squeezed between or beneath the cars, flattened in doorways, on the steps of the Palais de la Légion d'honneur, behind the Gare d'Orsay. CRS patrols, stationed at the inter-

section of the rue de l'Université and the rue de Lille, fell
upon the flanks of those who fled and confined the survivors
to the narrow street. Those who survived the bloody gauntlet
were met on the quai Anatole France with the emphatic
stutter of small-arms fire.

Behind the CRS and the gendarmes came a district company of intervention police. These men, officially entitled
Guardians of the Peace, played jackal to their paramilitary
colleagues, clubbing and kicking those of the wounded who
were unable to run.

One guardian of the peace noticed Nefissa and Hanna in
their doorway and ran at them, lead-lined cloak swirling,
truncheon upraised. Hanna saw that the man hesitated to
strike, and parried the blow before it fell: at the same time he
shouted in the *flic*'s face, "We're French." The *flic* hestitated.
Nefissa said, "That man is wounded," and pointed to the
young man crawling in the street. The Mussulman was
screaming: he was trying to drag himself along the pavement
with his hands. His face was like raw pluck: the eyes filled
with blood: no features: only a gaping mouth that screamed.
Nefissa started toward him. The *flic* transferred the truncheon
to his left hand and drew a small automatic pistol from the
patent leather holster on his right hip. He used the muzzle to
prod Nefissa in the uterus.

"Fuck off," said the guardian of the peace.

Hanna pulled her back and walked her up the street. They
had to pick their way among the wounded, whose screams
rebounded from the Second Empire façades. Some of the
wounded were silent, however; they lay in spreading pools of
blood. Nefissa clung to Hanna's arm: tears streamed down
her face, but she did not sob. She stopped by one man who
was propped against the wall, one leg at an odd angle, spaniel
eyes rolling.

"Can't we do something for him?"

"No."

She looked back down the street and Hanna turned his
head. The guardian of the peace had put away his pistol and

was standing over the crawling Mussulman with his truncheon. Hanna stopped.

A stocky policeman walked across the street and stood straddle-legged before them. He had a Sten-type MAT 49 submachine gun slung around his neck; he swiveled the weapon and poked the muzzle into Hanna's chest.

"Keep moving, monsieur," the *flic* said. "Keep moving, mademoiselle."

So they went back into the boulevard Saint-Germain. The *flics* had given up pursuit of the main body of Algerians. A section of the Gendarmerie nationale who had not yet been engaged were marching back to the *paniers-salades*.

"Just our luck not to have got at the *ratons*," one of them was saying.

"Let's get away from here," Hanna said.

"Yes," said Nefissa, "if we hurry we can overtake the column."

"I didn't mean that," Hanna said. "Haven't you had enough for one night?"

"My place is with them," said Nefissa. "Are you going to leave me?"

She took his hand: she was shaking and half running as though she would fall if she stopped moving. Hanna went with her and they soon overtook the decimated column, which had halted before the stone wall guarding the Ministry of Public Works and Transport. A small *panier-salade*, a Citroën T45 with corrugated sides, manned by five *flics*, was parked outside the Ministry. A young *flic* was standing facing the column with one foot on the running board. He looked like one of the figures in recruiting posters: broad-shouldered, wide-eyed, a trim black mustache. He was even smiling. He was holding one of the big MAS 50 automatic pistols in his right hand and it was braced on his left forearm.

The Mussulman column hesitated. Then the deputy leader, the man in the sheepskin jacket, led them forward, for the leader was gone with the melee. The *flic* fired. The impact of the fifty-millimeter bullet spun the deputy around; as he began to fall, a second bullet struck him with a noise like a butcher beating steak tender, and that shot brought him to his knees. Two of the young men in trenchcoats ran ahead and took him beneath the arms. They began to drag him across the road. His legs were dragging as though the motor muscles had given up. His tapered trousers were soaked in blood. He was making no sound at all. The *flic* was leaning against the *panier-salade* and laughing. All the *flics* were laughing.

The two lieutenants carried the wounded man across the boulevard Saint-Germain and into the rue Saint-Simon. There were still more than a hundred men left in the column, but they made no attempt to rush the five *flics*. They swarmed protectively about the women and children: Nefissa and Hanna went with them. Three of the *flics* followed and sealed off the rue Saint-Simon: the marksman with the MAS 50, flanked by two men with MAT 49s.

One of the trenchcoated young men had taken charge of the column: there was blood on his coat: he had been carrying the deputy leader. He was giving orders to two other young men who wore the civilian blue trenchcoat that was the uniform of the FLN hierarchy.

"Take Sidi Larba to the Red Cross in the rue de Sèvres," he said. "He's bleeding too fast to get him to one of our doctors. His spine has been hit, I think. Get the women and children to the Metro at Sèvres-Babylone. We'll double back into the boulevard Saint-Germain and draw them after us." He was speaking in French. Then he gave them his blessing in Arabic: "*Barake.*"

The parties divided but Nefissa marched with the men.

"You should go with the women," Hanna said. "I'll take you to them."

"I won't go with them. They are just wives. I'm a militant."

"You are a woman."

"I am a militant."

The new leader turned to ask what was the matter. He had a young face, pock-pitted and sad.

"This girl refuses to go with the women," Hanna told him.

"How dare you speak of me like that?" Nefissa asked. "You who are not even of us. I am a militant of the FLN and my place is with the column."

"Go with the women," the leader told Nefissa.

"No," she said. "I'm a militant. My place is with the column."

"Your place is to obey orders," the leader said.

"You are not of my cell," Nefissa said. " I don't take orders from strangers."

"I can't force you to leave," the leader said. "You will have to look after her," he added, speaking directly to Hanna. "*Barake.*"

"I'll do my best," Hanna promised.

"I can look after myself," Nefissa said. "I am a militant of my cell." But the leader had turned away.

"Where are we going?" Hanna asked, falling in step beside him.

"To the cafés of Saint-Germain. They won't dare to attack us in front of the intellectuals: the outcry would be too great."

"Isn't that rather a big assumption? Wouldn't it be better to disperse and go home?"

"That would give the *flics* an excuse for what they call a rat hunt: they would catch the wounded and the women. They would break into our homes and cafés. No, our only hope lies in solidarity: as long as there is a column still marching, the *flics* will follow it."

As they talked, the new leader was leading them through the back streets, so that they regained the boulevard Saint-Germain by way of the rue de Grenelle and the rue du Bac. The Mussulmans were dragging their feet: many of them were again barefoot.

The rain had ceased and was succeeded by a cold wind that blew down the length of Saint-Germain.

"I feel as though I were one of a column of black ants marching along the floor of a coffin," Hanna said suddenly.

"Just because you try to write verse in French there is no need to dispirit everyone with your morbid imagery," Nefissa rebuked him.

"It was a natural image that arose out of my own foreboding," Hanna said.

"Then keep it to yourself," Nefissa told him. "For us there can be no verse other than the poetry of political action. *Al-gé-rie, al-gé-rienne.*" She began to clap rhythmically.

No one took any notice of Nefissa; presently she stopped clapping.

They were retreating up the boulevard Saint-Germain by the opposite pavement to that by which they had advanced. They passed the Brasserie Lipp, the terrace a field of button-hole rosettes of the Legion of Honor, and the Royal Saint-Germain, where suburban youth gaped at them through an aura of fluorescence. There were now plenty of French people in the street: they stopped and stared at the bloodied, limping Mussulmans.

Hanna excused himself to Nefissa and crossed the road to a urinal: on the way back he saw that the column was being shadowed by a *panier-salade*. He drew the leader's attention to it.

"Pay no attention," the new leader said. "They won't dare touch us here, before their own intellectuals." Then he said, "By God, if only the FLN had allowed us to go armed. By God, it would not have been thus." He was speaking in Arabic.

Hanna, still looking back, saw that the first *panier-salade* had been joined by three more; he tightened his grasp on Nefissa's hand.

And as they crossed the rue du Four he watched the *paniers-salades* until they overtook the Mussulmans and disgorged *flics* to grapple themselves to the column. And again the column broke.

Hanna drew Nefissa into a crowd of French onlookers who were standing before a café. The French were crying long-drawn-out "Oooooh-ah," repeatedly.

"It is like listening to them watching the fireworks display on Bastille Day," Hanna said.

"Let me go," Nefissa said, but she did not struggle.

Some of the Mussulmans ran into the Mabillon Metro station; the railwaymen must have closed the platform gates, because the refugees were dragged out one by one and clubbed. The *flics* were all Metropolitan Guardians of the Peace. One, an officer from the way he commanded obedience, was in civilian clothes, but he bore a yard-long truncheon: a big man in a brown tweed jacket buttoned tightly over a heavy paunch, with cropped grey hair and a magenta beak of a nose. He chivvied the Algerians as a farmer chivvies a flock on market day; but without respect, for these human cattle had no value. He caught one Mussulman youth of about fifteen and beat him to the ground. He had to call two uniformed *flics* from a *panier-salade*—one of three blocking the western end of the rue du Bac—to drag this Mussulman away. The boy was bleeding from the ears. Then the farmer-like officer intercepted another lad who had been flushed out of the Metro and struck him across the face with his truncheon until the Mussulman began to spit blood. The uniformed *flics* had formed a double column along the street and the prisoners were being made to run the gauntlet of truncheon blows all the way to the *paniers-salades*. Those who fell were kicked to their feet; some, blinded by their own blood, went in circles and ran the gauntlet twice; the insensible were being dragged by their feet, face downward. One boy was marched along with a submachine gun at his back, instead of being subjected to blows. Then a second *flic* broke ranks, turned the Mussulman around, and smashed his head face downward against a parked car: the crunch of the nose breaking was clearly audible. His persecutor searched him, pawing deeply into the crotch; but there were no weapons and so they took the Mussulman away to the *panier-salade*. A *flic* was standing beside the vehicle: he was armed with a truncheon. Each time a prisoner climbed the steps, the *flic* hit him twice over the kidneys; when this happened the prisoner screamed and fell flat on the floor of the *panier-salade*.

There were Parisians at the windows of their apartments: they were shouting "Oooh-ah!"; there were Parisians on the pavement: they were staring; there were Parisians on the first floor of La Coupole overlooking the street: they were eating.

The white-faced major with the silver-braided kepi was back: he came up to the group in which Nefissa and Hanna stood. He wore a double row of medal ribbons: he was a Knight of the Legion of Honor.

"What are you all watching?" he asked them. "There is nothing to see. You understand. There is nothing to see. Go away. You are watching nothing."

They began to disperse. Hanna drew Nefissa with him, but she resisted.

"Let me go," she said. "I'm staying. My place is here with my people."

"Imbecile," Hanna said. "Triple idiot. Don't be an imbecile."

He got a wristlock on her arm and forced her to walk beside him. He forced her past the agonized voices in the *paniers-salades* and into the rue des Canettes.

"Stop it," Nefissa said. "You're hurting me." Tears were starting out of her eyes.

Something slapped Hanna's cheek from behind and he turned at bay in the angle formed by a café front, dragging Nefissa with him in a half circle. The white-faced officer confronted them; he dangled a right glove.

"Why are you hurting this young lady?" asked the major. "Won't she accompany you of her own free will?"

"She was upset . . ." Hanna began.

But the major said in a metal-rasp voice, as though his throat had changed down a gear, "I didn't ask you. I asked the young lady. Let go of her wrist at once."

The glove flicked across the tip of Hanna's nose; it began to smart, making him sniff saltily, and he dropped Nefissa's wrist.

Nefissa began to massage her left wrist with her right hand;

tears were running down her cheeks; her breasts began to strain against her black leather jerkin; she was pouting.

"What, has this peasant been hurting you?" asked the major. The glove again flicked across Hanna's face. Hanna made a move, then stopped. The flap of the officer's holster was tucked beneath the butt of his automatic pistol.

"What was he doing to you?" the major asked. "Come along, my dear. You can tell me. You have nothing to be afraid of now that I'm here."

Three screaming Algerians ran the police gauntlet.

"It was nothing," Nefissa said. "Nothing at all."

"It must have been something," the major said. One of the Algerians had collapsed and a *flic* dragged him by the ankle: his head went echoing down the roadway like a coconut toppled from its stand.

"You're not afraid of me, are you, dear?" asked the major.

"No," said Nefissa.

"Then why don't you talk?"

"We were having a tiff."

"A lovers' tiff."

"We are not lovers." She was looking down at the pavement beneath her feet.

"Then why are you quarreling?"

"The lady was naturally distressed at the sight of blood," Hanna began, but the glove flicked out like a leather tongue and he tasted blood upon his lips before he had finished speaking.

There were now two *flics* standing behind the major.

"I was speaking to this young lady," he said. "When I wish you to answer I will address a question to you." He turned to Nefissa. "I can't congratulate you on your choice of escort, my dear. But perhaps he wasn't of your choosing. Perhaps he was forcing his attentions on you under the pretext of helping you. Would you like to bring a charge against him? You have only to say the word. The police are your friends."

"No," Nefissa said. "He wasn't molesting me. He was trying to help me. He is my friend."

"Then why was he dragging you along?"

"He thought I should go away—as you ordered."

"And you didn't want to go. You wanted to stay with the Algerians."

"I wanted to stay."

"You look like an Algerian yourself, my dear. Tell me, have you been demonstrating with them? You can tell me, my dear. I shall understand."

"I protest," Hanna said. "I am a Lebanese citizen and I protest these questions. Here is my passport and my residence permit and my working card."

He put his right hand to an inner pocket to take out his dossier and found himself staring into the muzzles of the two MAS 35s that the *flics* had drawn. He did not complete the movement.

"Let him produce the papers," the major said. "This is becoming interesting. So you are an Arab."

He had begun to address Hanna as "thou."

Hanna produced his dossier and the officer tucked his gloves into his Sam Browne belt before taking it. He flipped quickly through the papers.

"It says here that you have applied for French nationality and that you have passed the first stage. It seems there is no objection to your naturalization. So you are one of us. Perhaps you were trying to restrain this woman's ardor. An ideological dispute." He turned back to Nefissa. "Are you a Mussulman?"

"Yes."

"She is assimilated," Hanna said. "Her father is a member of the administration in Algiers."

The major took out a notebook, made an entry in it, and allowed the elastic to snap on the cover before handing the dossier back to Hanna.

"Thank you, monsieur," he said. "You have proved that you are a good friend of France; no doubt you will prove to be an equally good Frenchman. How old are you?"

"I am twenty-seven," Hanna said.

"Then as a French citizen you will still be eligible for military service. You may soon be fighting these *ratons* in Algeria. We will deal with them here in Paris."

The major turned to Nefissa.

"Here are my papers."

The major thumbed through them.

"A student of the Sorbonne. You should confine yourself to your studies, mademoiselle. What course are you following, mademoiselle?"

"The law, officer. The French law."

"Indeed? No doubt you hope to be called to the Paris bar?"

"I hope to have that honor."

"And to plead the cause of dirty terrorists who are arrested in Algiers so that they shall enjoy the benefits of French justice, which they are trying to overthrow. Isn't that so, mademoiselle?"

The major's white face was suddenly beaded in sweat: his spectacles had misted over: he took them off and polished them with a handkerchief from his sleeve.

Nefissa said nothing.

"But justice isn't everything, mademoiselle. The instrument of justice is the police. Did they teach you that at the Sorbonne, mademoiselle?"

Nefissa said nothing.

"The police have a duty," the major continued. "It is their duty to interrogate suspects found in suspicious circumstances. I've done that. When the suspect is involved in a crime of violence—such as tonight's manifestation by your coreligionists—it is also their duty to search them for concealed weapons. I shall now do my duty."

"I protest," Hanna said.

The major rounded on him.

"Remember that you are about to become a French citizen, monsieur. Remember that your present livelihood and your future prospects depend upon France. Remember that French citizenship carries duties as well as privileges and that one of those duties is to assist the police. You may now do your duty by keeping silent and not interfering in a police investigation."

"But she's only a girl," Hanna said. "She should be searched by a woman, if she must be searched at all."

"That is a counsel of perfection, monsieur. We have no women available for the task. Would you ask that Frenchwomen should be exposed to the violence of a Mussulman mob? If she is to be searched by women, she must be taken into custody. Do you wish me to arrest her? If she has no concealed weapons, your friend has nothing to fear. I will let her go."

"I won't be searched by men," Nefissa shouted. "It's too humiliating. You just want to humiliate me. I shall scream."

"I doubt if your screams will attract much attention among so many," the major said. He smiled. "Seize her," he ordered the two *flics*.

The *flics* holstered their pistols and pinioned Nefissa's wrists so that she faced the wall with her arms behind her head. The officer's hands probed Nefissa's armpits and then ran down her body to waist level.

"Take your filthy hands off me," she shouted. "You filthy *flic*."

"It is an offense to insult the police," the major said. "As a law student, you should know that. Open your legs."

"No," she said. "Stop it. Stop it, you bastard."

"This is a regulation search," the major said. "Made before witnesses. It must be thorough."

When he raised Nefissa's skirt above the tops of her stockings, Hanna started forward and felt a hand upon his shoulder. There were two *flics* standing behind him. They were laughing, but they had drawn pistols.

"Remember that you are almost a French citizen now," said one of them, a corporal. "You can watch if you haven't seen it all before, but don't move."

"But it's disgusting," Hanna said. "Disgusting and degrading."

"Don't move," the corporal said.

Nefissa screamed once; she was straining to keep her thighs closed as the major's hand quested beneath her buttocks. The major stepped back and hit her twice behind the knees with the heel of his hand: when her legs gave he thrust his right hand into her crotch. Nefissa squirmed, then whimpered.

"There's something hard there," the major said. "And this time it isn't a penis. I know you Moslem virgins. It makes a convenient receptacle for everything, isn't that so, mademoiselle?"

Nefissa said something into the wall and cried out and said something more.

"Don't give me that, dear," the major said. "I was acquainted with the facts of life before you were born."

He removed his hand for an instant and tugged: Nefissa's briefs fell about her ankles: they were white, as though in token of surrender.

"Now we can resume the search," the major said.

Then Nefissa stepped free of the restricting nylon and elastic: she kicked backward and caught the major on the shin with her sharp leather heel: he said *"Merde"* and caught her by the ankle; his unfettered right hand thrust upward between her legs.

The major grunted and extracted something from between Nefissa's legs: he allowed the bloody cylinder of cotton to fall to the pavement.

"The investigation is completed," the major announced. He took the handkerchief from his right sleeve and wiped his fingers; then he returned it to his sleeve.

"You may go now, children," he told them. "You see that you have nothing to fear from French justice as long as you are innocent."

Nefissa began to run down the street: she ran as though she were bandy-legged, though Hanna had seen she was rather knock-kneed.

The corporal called, "You've left your pants behind, mademoiselle," and all the *flics* laughed.

The major said to Hanna, "You have proved that you have

the makings of a good Frenchman. Just a word of advice: next time go out with a French girl."

The *flics* had put away their pistols.

"And I would like to say something to you," Hanna said. "*Algérie—algérienne.*"

Then he ran after Nefissa; but there was no pursuit; only the laughter of the *flics*. He soon caught up with her. She was sobbing as she ran.

Hanna tried to take Nefissa by the hand. She struck him off. She had crossed the boulevard Saint-Germain and along the rue de Buci, slipping on the rubbish left by the street market, before he again overtook her.

"Keep away from me," she said. "Coward."

There were spots of blood between her feet.

"I did what I could," he said. "They had guns."

"Don't talk to me," Nefissa said.

She went on into the rue Saint-André-des-Arts and Hanna followed at half a pace.

Nefissa stopped and pressed the buzzer of her apartment. She stood there sobbing, her back to the wall, facing Hanna, while the door to the inner courtyard creaked open.

"Don't go, Nefissa," he said.

"Keep away from me," Nefissa shrieked. "You coward, you. You Frenchman, you."

Behind her Hanna saw the concierge come into the courtyard and stand with arms akimbo in the light from her door.

"I won't become a Frenchman, I promise you," Hanna said. "Nothing on earth would induce me to become a Frenchman after tonight. You heard what I said to them? I'll join the FLN and learn to fight the *flics* on their own terms. You must help me to join the FLN, Nefissa."

But Nefissa had seen the concierge, and ran into her heavy arms. The frog-ugly face of the concierge glared at him over Nefissa's heaving shoulder.

"I heard what you said," she croaked. "You ought to be ashamed of yourself, trying to involve a young girl in politics. Be off with you. You Algerian, you."

"Nefissa," Hanna cried.

"Don't cry, dear," the concierge said. "What's he been doing to you? Why, child, you're bleeding. Bleeding from there! You've been assaulted! Help! Police! . . ."

Hanna turned and ran. He fled down the medieval contours of the rue Saint-André-des-Arts and across the place Saint-André-des-Arts and he did not stop until he was once more in the place Saint-Michel. He stood in the shadow of the fountain and looked about him.

There was little to be seen: the broken windows of the Café de la Gare had been boarded up; the shattered scooter had been propped against a tree; the glass had been swept into the gutter; the shoes had been crushed to leather pulp by the passage of wheels; the rain had washed away the blood.

assassination

⊕ A man was lying awake in an unlit corner room on the second floor of the Hôtel de L'Univers et de la Chapelle. Beside him a woman slept. She was lying belly down, her mouth distorted by the pillow and agape with snores. The man was chain-smoking Celtiques: one crumpled blue pack was screwed up in the tin that served as an ashtray and there was only one cigarette left in the second pack. He took this and lit it carefully from the discarded butt. When the hands of his luminous watch pointed to five thirty he stubbed out the cigarette, raised himself on one elbow, and twisted slightly to look at the woman. She still snored. Her knees were drawn up so that her bottom made a hump beneath the blankets. He reached down and gave a sharp tweak to the tuft of hair that sprouted beneath her buttocks. The woman groaned but did not wake. The man got out of bed.

The man stood naked in the shadowed room: a caricature of himself drawn by tricks of light. He might have stepped from a medieval bestiary: drooping eyes and sharpened ears and slipshod chin; the chin roughened with a suggestion of beard, the lower lip shining with slobber, the black hair ruffled into tines. The man stalked rather than walked to the door, moving heavy shoulders and hungry loins.

He put on a blue gabardine trenchcoat, buttoned and buckled himself into it, and then stood a full minute listening to the subterranean explosions of his bowels, tensing his sphincter and diaphragm muscles as though fighting against a desire to defecate. Then he struck himself in the belly several times. His bowels continued to rumble. The man shrugged his shoulders, opened the door quietly, and stood listening. There was nothing to hear. The man went across the landing, guided in the darkness by the strengthening smell of urine, to the *toilette à la turque.* He placed his feet fastidiously on the footrests; but they were damp; then he tucked up the trench-coat and squatted over the excrement-encrusted hole in the porcelain and noisily relieved himself. All the while he held the watch before his face: it was twenty to six when he straightened up.

The man cleansed himself perfunctorily with part of the previous day's *Le Parisien libéré,* touched the chain but did not pull it. Then he padded back to the bedroom where he filled the bidet with cold water, straddled it, and completed his toilet with soap, using the left hand only. This done, he lifted the metal basin out of the bidet and poured the water against the side of the sink, as a good barmaid pours bottled beer against the side of a glass, so that it went down silently. He replaced the bowl of the bidet and went to the window.

The Hôtel de l'Univers et de la Chapelle stood on the corner of a triangle shaped like a grocer's wedge of cheese. The most acute angle was the eastern end, where the rue de Chartres met the frontage of the boulevard de la Chapelle. The shortest side was the steep rue Fleury at the western side: it ran into an X-patterned crossroads formed by the intersecting of the rue de Chartres and the rue de la Charbonnière, which rose diagonally from the boulevard to complete another wedge-shaped block pointing west. The Hôtel de l'Univers et de la Chapelle occupied a corner of this crossroads, which itself formed a Saint Andrew's cross at the base of the butte Montmartre. From his window the man could see the Byzantine dome of the Sacré-Coeur beyond the broken façades of the rue de la Goutte d'Or, which gave the district its name.

But the man was not looking up at the church: he was looking down as the December dawn brought light into the dark street.

With the dawn came the first wave of Mussulman workers on their way to the Gare aux Marchandises and the Gare aux Charbons, whose freight trains occasionally shook the flimsy walls of the hotel to their foundations. The booted feet of these workmen clattered a reproach at the shuttered windows of the street. A man came out of one of the buildings at the crossroads, blew his nose into the gutter, wiped his hands on a green baize apron, and began to take down the shutters of the Café-Restaurant Ali Baba.

The clang of the shutters brought a man from the entrance of the Hôtel de l'Univers et de la Chapelle. He was a short man, and looked foreshortened to the watcher at the window; the back of his head rose without contour from the nape of his neck; the round skull was thatched with flaxen hair all shot with grey. He walked very erect and acknowledged the greeting of the man in the apron with a hand raised to the point that might have been occupied by a visored cap, had he not been bareheaded.

Dawn also brought relief to the two Mussulman auxiliary police who were standing in a doorway opposite, where their dark blue battle dress merged with the shadows. A big *harki* had stalked up the street, silent upon the thick rubber soles of his oiled leather boots. One of the men was half turned away when the newcomer prodded him with the muzzle of his MAT 49 submachine gun.

"*Attention terroristes!*" he said.

The two *harkis* jumped and clicked off safety catches and turned to see the big man laughing at them.

"*Tu es mort,*" he told them. "*Tous les deux.*"

"*Va-t'en faire foutre,*" they told him, stamping silent feet.

The man at the window was watching this scene and could hear what passed because the foundations of the Hôtel de l'Univers et de la Chapelle had shifted and there were deep cracks at the top and bottom of the frame, though the window was closed. By standing behind the soiled curtains the man could see and hear most that took place in the short street.

"Mohammed Kacemi," the man at the window said as the big *harki* turned his broad olive face, barred by a fiercely repressed black mustache, to the street.

The man left the window for the center of the room: he looked at the woman in the bed: she was still asleep. He

delved into the left-hand pocket of the trenchcoat and drew
on a pair of cotton gloves; then, with his right hand gloved, he
took a military-pattern MAS 50 automatic pistol from the
other pocket. The weapon shone beneath a transparent film of
fresh oil; but the man checked the action of the magazine,
which held a clip of ten cartridges. Finally he switched off the
safety catch before replacing the clip in the same pocket.

Then he left the room, going silently down the worn
wooden stairs until his bare feet met the chill of the flagstones
in the hallway.

The receptionist's cubicle—which held only a chair, a desk
bearing the hotel register, a book printed in a language the
man could not read, and an ashtray swimming with blood-
flecked spittle—was empty. The double entrance doors stood
half open, so that the man in the trenchcoat was able to ap-
proach them while shielded from sight of the street. When he
had reached a position behind the closed door the man went
down upon one knee and lifted the flap of the mail slit: the
hinges looked rusty, but they moved easily, with a glint of
oil.

Through his oblong of vision, the man in the hall could
now see the big *harki*, whom he had named Mohammed
Kacemi, standing opposite in the doorway of a shuttered shop.

The *harki* had lit a cigarette and gummed it to the left-hand
side of his lower lip; his eyes were narrowed against the
smoke, but constantly shifting to follow the progress of
passers-by. His right hand was flicking the button of the MAT
49, which was slung over his right shoulder, from repetition to
automatic.

The man in the hall was shivering with the cold contact of
the flagstones through the cotton trenchcoat, but his hands
were steady as he took the MAS 50 from his pocket and
aimed it through the mail slit. Then he began to sweat from
the forehead: he had to brush his left gloved hand across his
forehead to keep the sweat out of his eyes. Then he used his
left hand to prop open the lid of the mail slit; aligned the

front sight and rear sight of the pistol; and in this manner shot the *harki* across the street, keeping his index finger pointed along the barrel, squeezing the trigger back into second pressure with his middle finger, so that all was over within seconds, save for the echo in his ears and the sting and smart of cordite in his eyes.

Without waiting to see the result of his fire, the man in the hall stood up and took a padded envelope, of the sort used for sending books by mail, from his left-hand pocket. The interior of the envelope was stiffened with cardboard. It was addressed to:

> Mlle. Nefissa Saddok,
> Hôtel de l'Univers et de la Chapelle,
> 1 bis, rue Fleury,
> Paris-18ème.

The envelope was stamped and appeared to have been franked. The man put the pistol into the envelope, sealed it down with his tongue, grimaced against the fishy-flavored adhesive, and put the envelope into the mailbox behind the door. The man did these things as though he did not see the actions he performed: he did them as though he had been drilled to do them.

Then he wiped the sweat out of his eyes, took off his gloves, and returned them to the pocket, half turned, hesitated, and looked through the mail slit. Then he recoiled.

Mohammed Kacemi was still on his feet. There was a little blood above the pout of his battle blouse: the door behind him was splintered; not all the fifty-millimeter bullets had found their target. The right-hand side of his body, which seemed unharmed, was still active. The fingers of that hand were fumbling for the safety catch of the submachine gun suspended from his right shoulder. The cigarette still smoldered on his lower lip.

A group of Mussulman workers had stopped opposite to him, their backs to the hotel. They were arguing as to what had taken place. Someone was saying that the *harki* swayed because he was drunk on duty; that he was twice a renegade in betraying his people by working for the French and his religion by taking alcohol.

"He was shot," a youth said. "I heard the shots. A whole volley. There were thirty or forty shots. Hand grenades, too."

"Don't talk silly," an old workman rebuked him. "If there had been shots and hand grenades they would have come from a car and no car has passed this way. The FLN always attack the Goutte d'Or in cars. That's why the police keep a cordon of *harkis* around the block day and night. You only heard a car backfiring."

"How could I have heard a car backfiring when you've just said there was no car?" the youth asked.

"Don't be so cheeky to your elders just because you're working in France," the old workman said.

"I wasn't being cheeky," the youth protested. "I was just repeating what you said."

An argument began: people took sides: the *harki* was no longer the center of attention, except for the man in the hall, who went on watching through the mail slit.

Suddenly the great bulk of Mohammed Kacemi sank to the knees. His head was still up: his marble gaze was upon the door of the Hôtel de l'Univers et de la Chapelle: his right index finger was locked in the trigger guard: perhaps death and determination petrified the reflex, for the muzzle flamed yellow and the noise was continuous, like that of rotten linen being torn across, until all twenty-eight rounds had been fired.

The bodies of the Mussulman workmen took the first bullets. As they began to fall, the man in the hall dropped the flap of the mail slit, turned, and began to run up the stairs. The last of the burst went high: bullets gored through the weathered wood of the door of the Hôtel de l'Univers et de la Chapelle and sped through the dank gloom of the hall to set stone chips flying about the bare heels of the assassin and to ricochet, rising angrily to spend themselves in the rotting plaster about him, so that thick grey clouds swirled about his head.

The man paused to blink away the dust and then ran on as the firing ceased and cries began. He plunged through the door of his room, ripped off his trenchcoat without regard for the buttons, flung it over a peg behind the door, and was back in bed as the woman awoke.

"What's the time, Mohammed?" she asked through a yawn.

"I am Georges," he corrected her.

She was still bemused by sleep.

"Georges, Georges," she repeated. "I don't know any Georges!" She giggled, "Let me have a look at you."

But the man began to kiss her eyelids: mascara made his lips smart, but he only grimaced and went on kissing her.

"I am Georges Hanna, my love. Don't you remember your Georges? I've been here before. I've been here twice with you. You must remember me."

The man called Georges Hanna said all this as though he were willing the woman to remember him.

"I remember you," she said. "You gave me too much to drink last night and I passed out."

"You said you wanted a drink," he reminded her.

"I'm always ready for a drink," the woman said. "Wouldn't you be ready for a drink if you had to go with Mussulmans who either don't drink or won't drink because they're afraid they won't get at least three erections during the night if they do? They think they're disgraced if they can't do that. Did you know? But you wouldn't know because you're a Christian. Mean devils, they are. It wouldn't harm them to buy me a drink, would it? It doesn't make any difference to what I can do."

"It did this time," he told her. "You snored all night."

"And didn't you do anything? That's a good one. You didn't do anything because I was snoring. Ooh, la-la, la-la, la-la! How chivalrous."

"I didn't want to disturb you," he said.

"That was nice of you," she said. "But I'll bet you want to disturb me now, don't you? Otherwise you won't pay, isn't that so? I don't know what was the matter with me last night. Truly I don't. I thought I could drink Casanis. How many did I have? I can drink a whole bottle of Casanis. You've seen me drink a bottle of Casanis, haven't you? No, of course, you wouldn't have done because I only do it when I'm off duty. Well—nearly a bottle. I wasn't drinking it without water, was I? That's bad for the eyes. I could do with a drink now. Have you anything to drink? I've got a hangover. What a head. That's funny, isn't it? I've never had a hangover before. Isn't that strange?"

"Come here," he said.

"No," she said. "Not until I've had a drink. I've got a hangover, I tell you. *Merde*, I could do with a drink. Then I'll give you a rare time. I shan't ask you for any money until I've done it. You know me. No, of course, you don't really know me, but you're going to know me. But not until I've had a drink. *Merde*, what are they making all that noise for? I can't stand it with my head. I've never had a hangover before— well, not really, because I can drink a bottle of Casanis without passing out. Shit, just listen to them. You'd think there was a war on. It reminds me of the Liberation. There was plenty to drink then, plenty of men to buy one a drink. *Merde*, I need a drink."

"I'll get you a drink," he said. "Don't get up."

"That's good of you, that is," she said. "I need a drink." She stretched out a hand and touched him: then she withdrew her fingers as though he were charged with electric current. "*Merde!* What's the matter with you. You're on fire. And you're shivering. You've got a fever. Are you sick?"

"No," he said. "It's nothing. There's nothing the matter with me."

She was propped on one elbow now and staring into his face.

"Jesus, Mary, and Joseph," she said, crossing herself beneath the sheet. "Your face is all covered with sweat. And you're white. What's the matter with you? Is it anything infectious?"

"There's nothing the matter with me," Hanna told her. "It's just that—well, I want you, you understand. I've been waiting all night, remember?"

"My God, you must want it badly. You must really want it badly. Let me feel you. *Merde!* You're limp. How can you want it so badly when you're limp? Have you shot your load into the sheets?"

"No," Hanna said. "Yes. Leave me alone."

"Don't be snob with me," she said. "You said you wanted me, didn't you? What the hell do you think I am? Your sister? What's all that noise about?"

"Just lie back and relax while I get you a drink," Hanna said. "Relax and close your eyes. I'll get you a drink and then you'll feel better."

He pressed her back to the pillow and again closed her eyes with the pressure of his lips: she allowed him to do so: she began to smile. When he saw her smile, Hanna got out of bed and went to the sink: his body was streaked with sweat. When he got to the sink he began to sway and had to steady himself by taking a grip on the cracked enamel bowl. There was a tooth mug in a bracket above the basin: he rinsed it carefully beneath the tap and shook out the drops of water. Then he walked to the bedside chair and took a bottle of Vittel water from a swag-bellied briefcase. The woman was watching him from the bed.

"You're a character, you are," she said. "Do you always carry a bottle of Vittel?"

"I wouldn't drink Paris water."

"Me, I wouldn't drink water at all. But fancy bringing a bottle of Vittel with you."

"Making love always makes me thirsty."

"But you haven't been making love."

"No, but I'm going to."

He was still sweating: the drops were running down him as he drank the first glass of Vittel: it was cold in the room and he refilled the glass and gave it to the woman. She took a sip and grimaced.

"Not for me. Rots your shoe leather, that stuff. I'm going out to get a proper drink before you start on me."

"Wait," Hanna said.

"What do you mean, wait? I need a *café-fine*. I tell you, I've got a hangover. Just listen to that noise. That's a *flic* car. Those sirens have a bad effect on my sinus and give me a headache. I'm going to have a *café-fine*. There goes another *flic* car. I wonder what's happening."

"There's always something happening in the Goutte d'Or," Hanna told her. "They're probably rounding up a few unemployed Algerians. They're always doing it."

"Well, they won't stop me getting my *café-fine*," the woman said.

She was sitting on the side of the bed now: her platinum blond hair fell in brittle strands from charcoal roots: by contrast her pubic hair was luxuriantly black and curly. The morning light revealed a pudgy face, like dough after the first kneading and with as many open pores; but the eyes were huge, violet, clear as marbles. Her body was going to seed: great amorous yet unfulfilled breasts were withering above the darkened, hair-encrusted, splayed teats, and sagging below; the long torso swelled into thickly cushioned thighs; and the short legs, hairy as those of a spider, were knocked at the dimpled knees. She had absurdly small feet, very dirty between the toes and beneath the nails.

Hanna, who was also standing naked, looking down at her, said nothing, and finished the water that she had rejected.

She stood up and stretched; bedewed black tufts sprang out of her armpits, giving the morning air a sweat-tang; her protuberant navel momentarily retreated as muscles moved somewhere behind the flab; a reticent fragrance of urine gave a dry bouquet to the cloy of sweat. And the man, Hanna, felt the sexual impulse rise within him until it tautened his limp penis.

"Do you like me?" she said. "I can see your friend likes

me." She slapped his penis. "But first I need a *café-fine*."

"Wait," Hanna repeated. "I can give you something better than a *café-fine*."

"Casanis?"

"Even better."

Hanna went to the chair over which his clothing was carefully draped. The trousers had their tops lying flat on the seat of the chair to support the weight in the two hip pockets. He took a flask from one of these and gave it to the woman. She unscrewed the stopper and placed her putty nose over the neck; she inhaled deeply; then she drank.

As she drank, the woman's body seemed to assume new form and life: her breasts heaved; stomach contracted; toes curled into the threadbare carpet. Her Adam's apple recorded three separate swallows before she stood up and, still holding the flask, put her arms about Hanna's neck and kissed him full on the mouth. Hanna averted his head slightly, but her sensuous, shapeless mouth sought and enveloped his lips; her rasping tongue began to grope within the intimate recesses of his mouth: her breath was like stale fire.

"Darling," she said. "That was marc. And such marc. I haven't tasted the like of that since I was a girl in Caen. You never bought that: it's more than fifty degrees."

"Eighty degrees," he said. "It was distilled on a farm."

"Angel," she said. "I'm half pissed already."

She released him and took another drink before handing over the flask. Hanna was shivering. He took a small drink from the flask and the shivering became worse. He took another drink from the flask and the shivering ceased. He had a third drink and handed the flask back to the woman. The shivering began again.

Outside in the street, they could hear the whomp and wail of another police car.

"You'd better get back into bed," she said. "You're cold."

"Yes, let's," Hanna said.

"I don't mind what you do to me now," she said. "I'll do anything you like. I feel delicious. I'll spend the whole day with you, if you like. I feel delicious."

She gave him back the flask and cupped her breasts in her hands; then she ran them down over her sagging hips and brought her fingertips together, so that they framed her pudendum.

"I feel delicious," she told him.

"Do you?" he said. "Let's go to bed. Let's spend the day in bed."

"You understand, don't you, that it will be additional to the night?" she asked, lifting her hands from her genitals and ticking off the points on the fingers of her left hand. "There was last night"—she recorded it upon her index finger—"and it was not my fault that you felt incapacitated because you gave me too much to drink, *Hein?* And there is this morning. And the whole day would mean the afternoon as well. If things go well, you will be exhausted tonight and in need of sleep." Her digital accountancy had now reached the little finger. "You understand that would count as four? That would be ten thousand francs for the four occasions because I might otherwise be out of business."

"That's all right," he said. "That's perfect."

"Have you any money?" she said.

"Yes," he said. He went to his jacket and took a note for one hundred New Francs from his wallet. "Here's your ten thousand."

"Thank you," she said. "That's the act of a gentleman, that is. I see that you are *sympathique.*" She put the note away somewhere within an enormous black plastic handbag.

"Let's go to bed," Hanna said. He was shaking all over now. "Quickly," he said. He took another drink of marc and flushed down to the collarbone.

"First I must pee-pee," the woman said.

"What's that?" asked Hanna, his lips still at the flask.

"I must pee-pee," she repeated.

"What is that?" asked Hanna. His eyes had turned blood-shot, and he was breathing cider brandy out of his mouth.

"I want to piss," she said. She lowered her eyes.

"Ah, now I understand," he said.

"I shan't be long, dearest," she said. "Can you wait?" She blew him a kiss.

"No," he said. "Don't go."

He put down the flask on the table and went to her: his hands ran down over her buttocks so that their bodies came together, contour to contour.

"Don't," she said. "You're pressing my bladder. Stop it. That's torture."

A police car started up with its siren wailing.

"Don't leave me," he said.

"I must pee-pee," she said, wriggling.

"Do it here," he said. "In the basin."

"Don't be disgusting," she said. "Why should I do that?"

"I don't want you to leave me."

"Not even to piss?"

"I want to . . . watch you. Don't you understand how I feel?"

"What's come over you? Last night you made me turn off the light before you'd take off your clothes."

"Did I?"

"Yes, you did. You said that intimacy was a private thing and should best be kept for the dark hours. You talked like something out of the Sorbonne."

"Perhaps I did. This morning it doesn't seem important any longer."

"It's important to me," she said. "A girl must have some privacy."

There was still a lot of noise in the street outside, but it was mainly the hubbub of excited humanity. Then he heard the wail of another siren, less strident but more urgent than that of the police cars: the note of an ambulance.

"You said you'd do anything for me," he said, pressing her again.

"All right, all right," she said. "If that's what you want. You're a queer one, you. I've never had anything like this before."

"No," he said. "Each one to his taste."

He could hear the ambulance braking in the street outside and the siren ceased its wailing.

She backed up to the basin, pouting. She stood on tiptoe and got one buttock over the rim of the basin, but flaccid flesh slipped on the stained porcelain and she came down hard on her heels.

"You'll have to help me if you really want me to do it," the woman said. "And hurry up, because I'm bursting."

He put the palms of his hands beneath her buttocks and lifted her easily: he had the depth of chest and breadth of shoulder of a long-distance swimmer: he was furred with black hair from collarbone to penis; he lifted her easily into the basin as she placed the flat of her hands on his shoulders and splayed her legs about his waist.

"Careful," she said. "The taps are digging into me. Lift me higher."

He obeyed, so that they were now gazing into each other's eyes, and showing the strain.

They stood thus for a full minute, she with contorted diaphragm, he with bulging muscles.

"What's the matter?" he asked, face reddened with the strain.

"I can't do it like this," the woman told him. "I'm too embarrassed."

He lowered her to the floor.

"All right," she said. "I wasn't built for athletics."

She crouched over the bidet, and as the enamel resounded to the discharge and the steam rose between her thighs, Hanna averted his eyes. The room was filled with the odor of escaping urine.

"I thought you wanted to see me do this," she said, rising and tipping the contents of the bidet down the sink.

"Yes," he said. "So I did, but I was embarrassed. I've never seen a woman relieve herself before."

"Well, you should have made the most of it," the woman said, running the tap briefly over the bidet before returning it to the stand on which patches of rust showed through the white paint. "It was no pleasure to me."

"A relief, perhaps," Hanna said and smiled.

There was no sound now from the street outside; even the voices had died away.

"Oh, stop standing there grinning," she said. "What did you make me do it for, if you didn't want to watch me? You students are all the same. Did you expect me to piss 4711?"

"I'm not a student," Hanna said.

"No, you're too old," she agreed. "What are you?"

"I was an airline officer," Hanna told her.

"Won't they want to know what you're doing away from your desk all day?"

"I left," he said. "I've joined a bigger organization."

He smiled again: there was still no noise from the street.

"Won't they miss you?"

"I don't have to report to them until tomorrow."

"Well, don't be so complacent about it," she said. "You office workers make me sick."

"I'm not complacent," he said. There was still silence in the street below. "Have another glass of marc."

"Well, why shouldn't I?" she asked. "Being shut in here all day with a character like you. I might as well have some pleasure for my pains."

"Why not?" Hanna said, handing her the flask.

"Shit," she said, handing it back to him. "That makes me feel better. That has what it takes, that stuff. Let's go to bed. I'm cold."

The flaccid flesh was pimpled now, like that of a freshly plucked fowl.

"Aren't you going to wash first?" he asked.

"What do you think I am: the public health department?" she asked. "Do you think I'm dirty? Perhaps you think I'm sick. What right have you to call me dirty?"

"I meant nothing," Hanna said.

"I suppose you'd like me to shave as well before we have a fuck? Is that it? I'm not one of your Mussulman bitches. Anyway, what's the matter with you? You're not even circumcised."

"I told you already: I'm not a Mussulman; I'm a Christian. But Levantine Christians observe some Mussulman customs."

"I don't care what you do."

In the street outside Hanna heard the ambulance start up and move off: it did not bother with the siren: the urgency was past.

"I'm sorry," he said.

"Let's get back into bed," the woman said. "I'm cold."

"Let's go," Hanna agreed.

But when they were again in bed together Hanna handed her the flask. She drank a great deal at one tilting draught and handed it back to him.

"Better make it last if we're going to be here the whole day," she said.

Both her diction and her eyes had lost something of their original clarity.

"It will," Hanna said. "It's a big flask."

"Are you trying to make me drunk?"

"Yes," Hanna said. "I'm trying to make you drunk so that I can seduce you."

"Oooh-la-la-la!" she said. "That shouldn't be difficult. Let's see what you can do."

Her right hand crept down beneath the blankets to his genitals; but his penis remained limp despite her massage.

"What's the matter?" she said, looking up sharply. "Don't you want it?"

Hanna was lying on his back, his hands clasped behind his head, looking up at the ceiling; he was sheathed in sweat.

"I'm sorry," Hanna told the woman. "I was thinking of something else."

"Do you mean that you're thinking of someone else?" the woman asked.

"Is that someone coming up the stairs?" Hanna said.

"What does that matter?"

"It matters to me," Hanna said.

They could hear the steps of two men mounting the stairs; there was a loud knock at the door.

"Open up," a man's voice said in guttural French. "It's the police."

"It's the police," the woman said. "I wonder what they want? They couldn't want to see me, not when I'm working."

"You have many friends in the police, haven't you?" Hanna said.

"Well, most of them are *harkis*, but there is a corporal at the police station. A Frenchman, who always asks for me."

The woman was pouting.

"Get a move on," someone was shouting on the other side of the door. "Speed it up."

"Aren't you going to answer the door?" the woman asked.

"No," he said. "You answer it. You know them all."

"Oh, very well," the woman said. "What a nuisance. Just as I was beginning to get comfortable."

The knocking at the door was renewed.

"Get a move on," the voice said.

"Just a second," the woman said, "I'm coming. Keep calm."

She got out of bed and stepped into her skirt; then she drew a tight woolen sweater over her head: she was just about to open the door when Hanna said, "Wait a minute till I get my trousers on."

"I thought you were going to stay in bed," the woman said.

"I'll feel better when I've got my trousers on," Hanna said.

"They won't cut it off," the woman said. "But they might just as well do that for all the use it is."

"What did you say?" Hanna asked, fastening the waistband of his slacks.

"I said get a move on," the woman said and opened the door.

Two squat *harkis* came into the room: the first man was a corporal; the second carried a submachine gun at the ready.

"Good morning, gentlemen," the woman said.

"Good morning, mademoiselle," the corporal said. Then to Hanna:

"Your name, m'sieu? Where are your papers?"

Hanna took his wallet from his jacket on the back of the chair and handed over his residence permit, working card, Lebanese passport, and another document from the Ministry of the Interior.

"So you are Lebani, Monsieur Hanna," the corporal said. "Do you speak Arabic?"

"I speak Arabic," Hanna said in that language, "but not your Arabic and not very well. French was my first language."

"*Christi?*"

"*Aiwa.*"

"It says here," the corporal said, reverting to his primitive French, "that you have passed the first stage of application for French citizenship."

"That is so," Hanna said.

"You're not a Mussulman?"

"I have told you, I was born a Christian," Hanna said.

"Good luck to you," the corporal said. He handed the papers back to Hanna, who put them carefully away in a special compartment of his wallet.

"Do you want to see my papers, Corporal Ahmed?" the woman asked.

"I've already seen your papers and a good deal more besides," the corporal said. He winked at her and laid a finger alongside his nose.

"Why, Corporal Ahmed!" the woman said. "Oooh, la-la, la-la. That's a nice thing to say!"

"But we must search the room," the corporal said, taking his finger away from his nose and drawing himself up straight. "We must search you, m'sieu."

"Oh, why must you do that?" the woman asked. "Can't you see that you've come at an inconvenient moment?"

"We must search the room for concealed weapons."

"There are no concealed weapons, officer," Hanna said. "Only this pistol."

He took a 7.62-millimeter MAB automatic from his brief-case; as he did so, the second *harki* brought up his gun, the woman uttered a little scream, and the corporal's hand dropped to his holster.

"Drop that," the corporal ordered.

Hanna's right eyebrow raised itself three lines above the left; but his face was otherwise in repose; he handed the pistol butt first to the corporal.

"Here is the weapon," Hanna said. "And here is my permit to carry it."

"Relax," the corporal shouted at the other *harki*. "Stop playing cowboys. Don't you know when a man is surrendering a weapon?"

"Not until it is out of his hands," the auxiliary said.

"That's enough," the corporal said. He broke the magazine of the MAB, but it was empty. He took out a pencil and a notebook: he tore a leaf from the book, wrapped it around the pencil, and poked it up the barrel. It came away filmed in oil.

"Here are the bullets," Hanna said. He opened a small cardboard box: it was filled with loose cartridges.

The corporal opened the breach of the MAB, inhaled deeply, and closed it again.

"The permit says that you are allowed to carry a pistol by reason of your job—is that so?" the corporal asked.

"That's right," Hanna said. "I work for an airline and I'm often on duty at night in an office where there are large sums of money and valuables."

"But you've given up that job now," the woman said. "You've got a better job with a bigger organization, haven't you?"

"Yes," Hanna said.

The corporal, who had been about to hand back the pistol and the permit to Hanna, arrested the movement.

"So there is no longer any need for you to carry a pistol, Monsieur Hanna?"

"I'm working for a travel agency now, but the conditions are the same," Hanna told him. "I work shifts and at night I am responsible for the safe."

"The name of the organization?"

"Mecca Tours."

"I have never heard of it," the corporal said. "You said it was a large organization."

"It is the most active in the Middle East," Hanna said. "It has only just opened a branch in Paris."

"Have you notified the police of your change of employment?"

"My employers are taking care of that," Hanna said. "They are taking care of everything."

"You had better write to the Ministry of Justice yourself," the corporal decided. "Then everything will be in order."

"Certainly."

"Just a formality."

"I understand."

"You can have your pistol back. And a word of advice: don't leave it lying about in a place like this: a pistol is a dangerous weapon if it gets into the wrong hands."

"I'll take care of it. To tell you the truth, I don't know much about firearms."

"I could tell that by the way you handed it to me. Be more careful next time."

"I will," Hanna said, putting the pistol away in his briefcase and restoring the permit to his wallet. "Thanks for the tip."

"Not at all," the corporal said. "Sorry to disturb you at such a time."

"Aren't you going to tell us what it's all about?" the woman asked.

"What? Didn't you hear anything?"

"Hear what? We've been asleep until ten minutes ago."

"Asleep because you've been at it all night and now that you've waked up you want to be at it again," the corporal said. He was smiling. "That's youth for you: I was like that at his age. Well, if you hadn't been so busy you might have heard one of our men being shot beneath your window not an hour ago."

"How awful!" the woman said. "Outside this very window, you say?"

"Well, just across the street anyway," the corporal said.

"Is that right? My God! Do you remember, we heard all that noise outside just after we woke up, Mohammed?"

"Georges," Hanna said. He was sweating again.

"Georges then. Do you remember the noise and the shouting?"

"I remember," Hanna said.

"But one hears so many incidents around here," the woman went on. "One gets used to it. But it isn't every day that a man is killed. Who was it, Corporal Ahmed? Was it anyone I know?"

"You knew him," the corporal said. "It was Mohammed Kacemi."

"Kacemi?" the woman repeated. "Kacemi, I knew Kacemi. That was a man."

"Perhaps he was too much of a man," the corporal said. "And perhaps that is why he is dead."

"What do you mean?" the woman asked. "Too much of a man? A woman can never have too much of a man like that."

"Perhaps men had had enough of him," the corporal said.

"Oh, politics," the woman said. "I don't think he bothered his head about politics. He did his duty."

"Not politics," the corporal said. "War. That was his job."

"What sort of a man was he?" Hanna asked.

"He was a man," the woman said. "You wouldn't understand. He was all male."

"He was very proud of being male," the corporal said. "He was so much a male that he sometimes forgot he was a man."

"I won't hear a word said against him," the woman said. "He's not here to defend himself."

"What sort of man was he?" Hanna asked.

"You know the type," the corporal said. "He was stronger than most men and he could satisfy most women. I don't suppose he ever had a thought in his head. He lived by instinct. I don't think he knew why he was wearing French uniform. He was a good *flic*."

"A *flic*," the woman said. "You're a fine one to talk about *flics*. You're a *flic*. You wouldn't have dared talk like that if he'd been alive."

"Yes. I would," the corporal said. "I was his superior."

"His superior? You weren't even his equal."

"I wasn't his equal as a *flic*," the corporal said. "I was a better policeman. I believe that terrorism should be left to terrorists."

"You'd better get the terrorists," the woman said, "then you can talk. Then you can be proud of your stripes."

"Kacemi got them," the corporal told her. "That was like old Kacemi. His reactions were slow, but he always got there in the end. He got the people who got him. There were at least eight of them, disguised as workmen. He killed an old man and a boy and wounded four more. He shot them as he was dying. Trust old Kacemi: he was strong like a bull. A group of them must have come past him so that he wouldn't be suspicious and then one or more of them shot him. The only thing we haven't found is the weapon."

"What weapon?" Hanna asked.

"The weapon that killed him," the corporal replied. "It must have been a nine-millimeter pistol. The police surgeon is examining him now, but I could tell the caliber when I saw the wounds. Those big bullets go through a man like a meat skewer—even a man like Kacemi. I knew what the weapon was as soon as I saw him. I was a scout in the French Expeditionary Corps in Italy, you know. I've seen what German nine-millimeter bullets can do to a man."

"So you still haven't found the man who fired the shots?" Hanna asked.

"I think we have," the corporal said. "Probably it was one or two of the wounded. But they must have passed their pistols to accomplices and hoped to slip away in the crowd. That's why we're searching this hotel. We want to make sure that no one slipped in here with the pistols."

"We were in bed at the time," the woman said.

"I know that," the corporal said. "I've already seen your names in the register."

"Then why bother to come and question us?" the woman asked.

"You might have been hiding something or someone," the corporal said. "Do you think I wear these stripes to match my complexion? I check up on everyone."

"Kacemi wouldn't have wasted time asking questions," the woman said. "He would have taken action."

"That is why he is dead," the corporal told her. "Now, since we both have better things to do, I must leave you. You are a young man, Monsieur Hanna: ten minutes under you and she'll have forgotten all about Kacemi. Go to it. So long."

The two *harkis* went out of the room, the man with the submachine gun walking backwards as though by instinct. The woman began to shout:

"*Bête! Bougre! Con! Bougre de con!*" She stopped as the door shut and put a hand to her head. Then she rushed to open it and shouted up the stairs, "Corporal! You were badly brought up."

She slammed the door and swung around with her back to it, panting, like a repertory actress registering emotion.

"Give me a drink," she commanded. "I need a drink. I want to get the taste of that prick out of my mouth."

"Why not?" Hanna said. He was smiling. He took the flask off the bedside table and unscrewed the stopper. He was still smiling, but, as he began to pour, the neck of the flask began a tarantella against the gunmetal cup; some of the marc spilled on the floor. He handed the cup to the woman and more marc spilled on the floor.

"Christ," the woman said. "Don't waste it. What's the matter with you now?"

Hanna sat down on the bed: he drank the marc straight from the flask, tilting it until his head was back and sweat sprang from his temples, which were suddenly hollowed, and when he set down the flask his face was highlighted above the bone, as though the flesh had been flayed, and it was no longer a French face, but Oriental, as though a mask had been peeled away.

"That's better," he said. "I feel better now."

"Let's go to bed," the woman said.

"Have you no respect?" Hanna asked.

"Respect? Respect for whom?"

"Respect for the dead." He raised the flask to his lips. "Let us honor the dead."

"You're drunk," she said.

"Let us drink to the dead," Hanna repeated.

"I've got nothing left to drink," the woman said. She held out the gunmetal cup.

Hanna was catching the last drops from the inverted flask with his tongue. Some of the drops missed his mouth and trickled from his chin to mingle in the sweat-beaded hair on his chest. The room reeked bitter-sweet with marc: it was overpowering the sick-sweet smell of their bodies and the stale-sweet smell of all the cigarettes that Hanna had smoked in the night.

"So you won't drink to the dead?" Hanna asked the woman.

"There's nothing left to drink," the woman pointed out.

"I could think of worse ways of passing the time than in drinking to the glorious dead," Hanna said.

"I could think of better."

"You've got no respect for the glorious dead, for the *harki* Mohammed Kacemi, Croix de Guerre, Palme en Bronze, *assassiné par un terroriste, mort pour la France.*"

"Don't be a cunt," the woman said.

"I don't intend to," Hanna said. "That's why I'm inviting you to drink instead."

"You keep saying that, but there's nothing left," the

woman complained. "You've drunk everything."

"That's what you think," Hanna said. "I know better. There's more than pistols in that case."

He went to the briefcase and took out a full bottle of marc; the bottle was unlabeled. He set it on the table and took a folding corkscrew from the case. He inserted the corkscrew diagonally and then set the bottle between his knees and pulled steadily so that the cork came cleanly away, leaving no vestige in the spirit.

"Do you always carry so much alcohol with you?" the woman asked. "Or aren't there enough cafés in Paris to satisfy your thirst?"

"I was going to give a party," Hanna said. "A party to celebrate my new job."

"You won't have anything left for the party at the rate you're going," the woman said as she took the bottle.

"We'll have a party here," he said. "Just you and I."

The woman took the bottle from her lips to say "Suits me," and drank again.

"Let's drink together," Hanna said. He slopped some marc from the bottle into the flask and handed the bottle back to the woman. He stood up very straight, holding the flask before him at arm's length. "Let us drink to the glorious dead."

"Do you mean that?"

"Of course I mean it," Hanna asserted, still standing at attention. He was swaying and sweating, but the flask was steady.

"He used to drink although he was a Mussulman," the woman said. "I don't suppose he'd mind us drinking to him. Anyway, he's dead. The dead are dead, I say. We came out of nothing and we'll go back to nothing. That's what I say."

"You should think before you speak," Hanna said. "There is no plant without a seed and old plants enrich new soil. I'm not even sure that death exists."

"Come to the window. I'll show you whether or not death exists. Did you hear what the corporal said? There are three dead men lying outside the hotel."

"I don't want to see them."

"You want to drink to them, but you don't want to see them," the woman said. "You deny death, but you don't want to look upon it. What sort of a man are you?"

"I am a man who likes to drink in peace," Hanna said, raising the flask.

"Have you ever seen a dead man?"

"Oh, yes," Hanna assured her. "I saw many dead men on the seventeenth of October. And I saw men being killed, which is worse."

The woman walked to the window and looked down into the street. Then she drew aside the net curtain and turned to Hanna. The face she turned to him was not like the face that had gone to the window. That face had been soft, putty, indeterminate: the first draft for a face on an art student's sketching pad. The face that turned from the window was expressed in the eyes, which were afire, and in the nostrils, which were flared, and in the mouth, which was enlarged.

"You should come and look," she said. "You're going to come and look before I drink with you. You are going to come and look before I will even fuck with you."

"It's too late," Hanna said. "The bodies will have been taken away."

"No, it isn't too late," the woman contradicted. "I can see all the bodies from where I stand."

"I don't want to see them," Hanna said.

"Are you afraid of the death you don't believe in?"

"It's not that."

"Well, come and look at the bodies. There are plenty of people looking at them. It doesn't take much courage to look at a dead man."

"Are people looking out of the windows? Are there a lot of people looking?" Hanna asked.

"Yes," she said. "What would you expect? It's a free spectacle."

"Then I'll look," Hanna said.

They had taken away the wounded: only the dead remained. Kacemi had been turned over so that he lay on his back; he was being examined by a man in an English-style blue suit who had a black bag on the pavement beside him: clearly the police surgeon. When he had finished the examination, the surgeon stood up and two *flics* covered the body with a blanket. The two Algerian workmen, the old man and the youth, were still lying uncovered on the pavement before the entrance to the Hôtel de l'Univers et de la Chapelle. There were four *harkis* with submachine guns forming a square about the bodies. A group of black-robed Algerian women, several of them tattooed on the temples, were kneeling with a cry that sounded like "Yo-yo-yo, yo-yo-yo, yo-yo-yo." Some Municipal *flics* were trying to move them on, but the women kept returning. Elsewhere *harkis* were keeping the curious on the move: the street was full of *harkis*: there was a line of them at either end of the street and more stopping and searching cars at the crossroads. In the midst of operations was a major of the intervention police, livid-faced beneath a silver-braided kepi and behind steel-rimmed spectacles. A sergeant stood beside him: he was a handsome *flic*, the black mustache trimmed to a sneer, like a face in a police recruiting poster; his stripes were spotless: he had been newly promoted.

The military-looking man whom Hanna had seen leaving the hotel at dawn was standing outside the Café-Restaurant Ali Baba with a glass of yellow-white liquid in his hand.

"Who's that man?" Hanna said, pointing to him.

"Him? Oh, him. Don't you remember? He's the night clerk."

"I know that. I asked you who he is."

"He's the old cow's lover."

"What old cow?"

"The *patronne*. Who do you think? She calls him her husband. Perhaps he is her husband: why else would a man live with an old cow like that? The way she treats us girls. I could tell you things about her that you wouldn't believe."

"No doubt, but I'd rather you told me things about that man."

"What is there to tell? The old cow treats him like dirt. She treats everyone like dirt. What a bitch."

"Why does he allow her to treat him like dirt?"

"Because he can't get another job when he's spitting blood all the time. It's disgusting. He drinks, too."

"So I see. But that still doesn't explain who he is. He doesn't look like a night clerk. He doesn't look like a Frenchman. Who is he?"

"A Pole. He has a bad chest. He's always drunk after six o'clock in the morning. Every morning the same. Pissed as a Pole, as they say. As soon as the Ali Baba is open. The old cow says he is an aristocrat and a captain, but he's just a miner. Anyone can tell that. All Poles are miners. They do the jobs that Frenchmen won't accept. No Frenchman would sleep with that old cow. A Frenchman wouldn't soil his prick in that old cow."

"So he was a soldier?"

"A soldier? That one? He was no soldier. A legionnaire more like. These foreigners join the Legion in order to obtain French nationality and do honest Frenchmen out of their jobs."

"I thought you said no Frenchman would do his job."

"Stop arguing. You're another foreigner so you wouldn't understand. Something is happening. Look."

Down in the street the major was talking to the police surgeon: he was talking with his hands. The right hand was uppermost and was descending from above his head; the left hand was traveling parallel to the ground. The surgeon was shaking his head. The major dropped his left hand and moved his right hand over the trajectory the left hand had traced. The surgeon began to nod. He moved his own right hand at the same level, but in a sharply rising gesture; then he reversed his hand and locked the thumb back over the little finger, so that only the three middle fingers remained pointing at himself. The fingers touched his chest, collarbone, and left shoulder. The surgeon's fingers were of eloquent length.

"Look," the woman repeated. "He is describing how it happened. I'm going to raise the window so that I can hear better."

"No," said Hanna. "It will attract attention."

The woman hooked her forefingers beneath the metal clasps of the window, but Hanna, who was standing behind her, reached around and leaned upon her hands.

"I want to hear what they're saying," the woman said. "Stop it. You're hurting me."

"I know what they're saying," Hanna said.

"You think you're clever," the woman said. "How can you know what they're saying?"

"I can see what they're saying," Hanna told her.

"But I want to hear them say it."

"No, it would only attract attention."

"What does that matter? We have a perfect right to be here, haven't we?"

"Have we? I thought whorehouses were illegal. The major might not be as understanding as your friend the corporal."

"All *flics* are understanding when they want something. The police allow houses in Chapelle because we are the only people left they've got any tags on. Most of the people around here are North Africans and the French are all Communists. Mean bastards. A girl can hardly make a living. And we're not breaking the law by being in a hotel room together. This is a hotel, you know. Anyone can stay here. Only last week we had a girl staying here who was quite the little lady, even though she was an Algerian, and she still calls here for her mail. Anyone can book this room. I don't live in it. You should see my room. You should see the room the old cow lets to me. Do you know the rent she charges for it?"

"Shut up," Hanna said. "They're talking again."

"There you are, you want to hear what they're saying only you're afraid to open the window," the woman said. "Well, I'm not frightened of them."

Hanna had relaxed his pressure on the woman's hands when she protested and now she suddenly heaved upward: the lower half of the window went up with a crash. In the street the major stopped speaking and looked up; in the same instant the sergeant drew his MAS 50 and aimed it at the window. The woman screamed, but without conviction.

"Don't shoot, officer," she said. "We were only curious. The police have already checked this room."

"At your service, mademoiselle," the major said. He raised his right hand, white-gloved, to the silver-encrusted peak of his kepi.

"Thank you, major."

"And tell that man to stop hiding behind you and come out where we can see him."

Across the street two *harkis* raised their submachine guns to cover the window.

Very slowly Hanna moved from behind the woman and stood framed in the window. He kept his head up, so that the upper part of his face was hidden by the centerpiece of the window frame. He stood quite still; he said nothing; his hands were at his sides, the palms turned outward, and they were empty.

"All right," the major said. "He's not armed."

The major turned away, the sergeant holstered his automatic, the two *harkis* lowered their guns. The major spoke to the sergeant and pointed to the military man, who still stood before the Café-Restaurant Ali Baba, drinking from his glass.

"What's his name?" Hanna asked.

"I don't know," the woman said. "I don't know anyone above the rank of corporal." She giggled. "I'm not that well in with the police."

"Not him," Hanna said. "The night clerk. The Pole."

"Oh, him. Why are you so interested in him? You're not turning pederast, are you? Is that why you find it so difficult with me? Are you a fairy trying to reform?"

"What's his name?"

"I don't know. One of those difficult names that Poles have. Sozanski or something of the sort. He's not camp. He drinks Casanis all day but he's not camp, though I wouldn't blame him, having to sleep with that old cow, not that he gets much time to sleep with her, being on the desk all night and drinking all day. I expect that's why he does it: so as not to have to sleep with that old cow, and I don't blame him."

"Shut up," Hanna said. "I want to listen to this."

The major was asking Sozanski, "Did you see what happened?"

"I did not see the *harki* shot. I heard the shots and came to the door. I saw everything that happened after the shots." Sozanski spoke French very well.

"Did you see anyone running away?"

"Everyone began to run after the *harki*'s bullets struck the crowd, but the sentinels stopped them at the crossroads."

"Did you see who he was aiming at?"

"I got the impression that he was aiming at the door of the hotel. He covered it for quite a long time before he was able to fire. That was because of his wounds. But he wasn't trying to aim at anyone in the crowd."

"Are you sure he wasn't aiming at the boy? The surgeon thinks the bullets entered on an upward trajectory, so it would seem that the boy was the assassin, since he's the shortest and he might have fired from the hip, while hiding behind the old man. But we can't find the weapon on either of them, nor among the others, although the *harkis* arrested everyone in sight. And the bullets came from a heavy-caliber automatic pistol, probably a MAS 50. It wouldn't be easy to conceal."

"I can only tell you what I saw, officer."

"Well, repeat it to me in detail. Not here. The whole street can overhear us. In the café. It seems to be a favorite resort of yours."

"That's right."

"Let's go there." The major turned to a lieutenant: "You take charge here, Pauvert. I want the whole block to be sealed off. I have the feeling that our man is still on the scene. You can clear away the bodies now: we've learned all we can from them. And I want barricades set up on the Chapelle, Marx Dormoy, Barbès, and Rouchouart boulevards: all cars to be stopped and searched. You won't find anything, but a show of force will impress the public. Show them they can't get away with shooting a *harki*. And when the *harkis* have finished checking the hotel, tell them to bring the register to me in the café. And get those wailing women out of the way." He turned to the sergeant: "You, come with us to the Ali Baba and post two men with guns outside. We don't want another assassination before we've solved this one. Now, Monsieur Sozanski, permit me to buy you an *apéritif*."

The woman turned to Hanna: "The *flics* are very generous with public money when they want information, aren't they? Fancy inviting that drunkard to have an *apéritif*. There'd be more justice if he invited some honest citizens instead of scaring the piss out of them."

Hanna had already returned to the flask on the bedside table. He lowered it to say, "Why worry? We've got plenty of our own alcohol. We'll see the *flics* again soon enough."

"Why should we? They've seen us once. What's it got to do with us anyway?"

"Have another drink."

"Help me get this window down. It's jammed."

"Leave it. I like the fresh air." Hanna was sweating again.

"Well, I don't like currents of air."

"That's because you're French."

"If you're going to be insulting . . ."

"I'm not. I just like to have the window open."

"What about me? Don't I matter? What if I catch the flu?"

"We'll be able to hear better with the window open."

"But they've gone to the Ali Baba."

"Have a drink and stop whining."

"Don't shout at me."

"I'm sorry. Get into bed and have a drink. You'll soon be warm."

"Oh, all right."

The woman took off her skirt and sweater, took up the bottle, and got into bed with it. She had a drink sitting up, shivering against the rawness of the air and of the spirit, and then held the bottle upright between her thighs while she drew the coverlet about her shoulders.

"Don't you wish you had one like that?" she said to Hanna.

"I'm quite satisfied with what I've got," he said. He was drinking steadily now.

"Well, I'm not satisfied," she said. "Aren't you going to get into bed with me?"

"Very well," he said, lifting aside the clothes.

"Not with your trousers on, stupid."

"I prefer it that way."

"Oh, my God, is this another of your preferences? I thought I knew something about men, but I've never met a man like you before. Do you prefer it with your clothes on? My God! What next?"

"I might want to get up in a hurry."

"So what? Your trousers aren't a kilometer away, are they? You have only to stretch out and pull them on. You're not going to wet the bed next, are you?"

"Shit!" he said. "Stop nagging me."

"I will if you'll stop acting so strangely."

"I'm not acting strangely," Hanna said.

But he got out of bed and turned the key in the lock of the door. Then he picked up the chair holding his other clothes and put it beside the bed. Finally he dropped his trousers, folded them carefully, and placed them beneath the briefcase. Then he got back into bed with the flask.

The woman had been watching him without speaking, without even taking another drink from the bottle.

"My God," she said. "What a man. You do everything as if it were predestined. You're more like a machine than a man."

"Oh, no," Hanna told her. "I believe in free will."

"My God," she said. "I didn't come to bed with you to discuss theology."

"The difficulty is," continued Hanna after taking another drink from the flask, "that, having exercised freedom of choice, one becomes a prisoner of decision. One is no longer free-willed, but self-willed. It is sometimes hard to become reconciled to the consequences. Now, if all were predestined, a man in my position could accept his destiny passively."

"And what is this choice you are talking about?" the

woman asked. "Not that I care. You bore me."

"Why? I am a man who has chosen to spend the day in bed with you."

"So I'm not good enough for you now, am I?" she said. "Well, get up and find someone else. I've had enough of your insults."

"It isn't a question of your not being good enough for me," Hanna said. He shook his head steadily and took another drink out of the flask. "You are far too good for me. I'm sure you have far less on your conscience than me."

"Are you making fun of me?" the woman asked.

Hanna hiccuped and excused himself: a delicate tracery of blood lines had spread about his irises; stubble sprouted from the swart places upon his chin and upper lip, nourished by a sweaty dew; his full lips were beginning to crack and he moistened them with a tongue that seemed to have been planted with yellow fur before he spoke again.

"Yes, I'm playing a game and the stakes are all I have."

The woman's lower lip came forward and her nostrils distended as she snorted, like a boxer, before delivering a roundhouse slap that stung his left cheek and spilled some marc on his bare chest.

"Swine," she said. "Son of a bitch."

"Don't do that," Hanna said. He was speaking thickly now, the furred tongue making an opening for the words through the cracked lips. He turned toward the woman so that she could see one cheek livid, the other imprinted with the slap that stood out like a birthmark. "I don't like violence," he said.

"I don't care," the woman said. "I'm glad I hit you. I'd do it again. I'm sick of your games. Sitting there and talking intellectual nonsense that no one but yourself can understand. You're just laughing at me."

"I do assure you that I'm not laughing at you. I'm laughing at myself."

"It comes to the same thing. You're laughing at yourself for being with a woman like me. You lie in bed getting drunk because you'd rather do that than make love to me. Isn't that it?"

"What are you grumbling about? You've been paid, haven't you, and you don't have to do anything for your money."

"So you think I care for nothing but money."

"Well, the sexual act can hardly be important to a whore."

"The act may not be important, but the man can make it important."

Hanna set down the flask on the bedside table and turned on one elbow to look at the woman. His fissured lips hung open: drink-staled breath came in gusts. He was trying to focus on the woman who was now cowering beneath the coverlet.

"What do you mean?"

"Hit me."

"What?"

"Hard."

"I don't want to hit you."

She dropped the coverlet and arched her back until it gave some support to her sagging breasts: ribs suddenly appeared from the flaccidity of her torso.

"You don't think of me as a woman at all, do you?"

"Well, I can see you're not a man."

Hanna began to laugh, looking down at her, raking her from navel to eyes; and when he met the eyes he stopped laughing and waited for what she had to say.

"Do you think that a whore lacks a woman's pride in her attractions? Do you think she takes pride in being rutted by men who have the sexual appetite of animals, using her as they would use a urinal, even though she may find pleasure in it? I don't know why you brought me to this room, but I do know it was not to fuck. That is why I want you to fuck me."

"So I'm a challenge to your professional pride, am I?"

"You understand nothing, do you?" the woman said. "You are an intellectual, but you are not intelligent. I am, let us say,

ten years older than you; looks I never had, and now my body
is going. It was a good body while it lasted. You can imagine
the sort of men it attracted. But occasionally there were men
who came to me in spite of themselves. There were men like
you. Perhaps they were not quite like you. There is something
about you that I do not understand. You have been lying here
with me a night and part of a day and nothing has happened
between us. And yet you have slept with me before and all
was as it should be. But if you did not bring me here for that,
why are you here? If you wanted a younger woman, there are
plenty of girls across the way in the rue de Chartres: teen-
agers with hard bellies and tight cunts. But you chose me.
You chose me for a night and you are keeping me for a day.
And still you cannot do anything. You are not even attempt-
ing to do anything. You're just lying there and getting drunk.
But I was the one you picked out: there are plenty of whores
in the Goutte d'Or, but you chose me. And you've picked me
twice before and not found me wanting. So you came to me
again last night to satisfy your need. So one of us must be at
fault. I know you're not impotent and you're still not too
drunk for sex. So if it isn't your fault, it must be that I am no
longer desirable to a young man like you, a man of passion
rather than a man of sex, a man who would only come to a
woman like me if he was driven to do so. Now do you understand why I want you to make love to me? Do you understand
why I slapped you? Do you understand why I wanted you to
strike me? Do you? Do you understand anything? Do you
understand what I want from you?"

"Yes," Hanna said. He could look steadily at the woman
now. "I understand. And I'm going to prove you wrong."

Then he kissed the woman and mounted her and they fused
into as great a two-backed beast as Rabelais could have de-
scribed and suddenly the woman screamed and screamed
again and went on screaming and Hanna gasped and groaned
and gave and it was over and they lay together as though
slain.

Hanna fell asleep, but the woman only dozed beneath his

bulk, holding his head tight beneath her cheek as he began to switch and mutter, moving her legs occasionally for relief from the pains of cramp, but holding him always. And the attitude of Hanna began gradually to change: the head sank, the arms thrust down between the knees, and the legs were drawn up; so that he went to sleep in the act of creation but awoke as though about to be born. And he slept muttering "*Avancez*," but he awoke with a cry of "*On les aura!*" uttered in the voice of another.

"The poor one," the woman said. "I didn't know he had been a soldier."

She stroked his head and then saw that his eyes were open. As he awoke his body began to change again: the joints flexed while the muscles stiffened and his whole being tensed: it was like watching the awakening of a cat. From slumber the man had become sentient, then supple. His right arm extended beneath the bedclothes, reached out to the chair, and touched the briefcase; when his fingers were resting upon the fiber fabric, his right arm withdrew, and his fingers touched her face and pushed back a strand of hair that had fastened upon her forehead in their heat.

"Why did you make me do that?" Hanna asked.

The woman looked into his face for a long time before she replied, "I told you. Have you forgotten already?"

"I see."

"So you do remember?"

"Yes."

The woman looked at him again and then she put both arms about his neck and drew his face down and kissed him on the lips, not deeply, but simply, so that the kiss was just a kiss and no observer could have judged its significance.

"Thank you," she said.

"Not at all."

After that they said nothing more for some minutes until the woman spoke again.

"Do you regret it?"

"Yes."

"Who is she?"

"A girl."

"Your wife?"

"No, I'm celibate. That is, say I'm a bachelor."

"Your fiancée?"

"No."

"What is her name?"

All the man's muscles became taut and he looked to right and to left without turning his face from the woman.

"It doesn't matter."

"Do you love her?"

"I don't know."

"I think you do. Do you know what I think? I think you brought me here to prove to yourself that you could resist me for her sake. As a sort of love test like one reads about in books. And I won."

"You're a romantic," Hanna told the woman.

"And you, I suppose, are a realist? Have you slept with her?"

"No. Not really. I suppose not."

"She's keeping both legs in one stocking until you propose, is she, the calculating little bitch. A prick-teaser. I suppose she tried to make you live up to a vow of celibacy. But I made you break it. I bested her. I'm glad of that."

"Why?"

"Because I'm a woman," the woman said. "I'm still a woman."

Hanna again stretched out his right hand and took a fresh pack of Celtiques from his briefcase: he pulled the red band that released the transparent top of the pack, tore off a corner of the silver paper, tapped a cigarette up from the bottom of the pack and into his mouth. He was reaching out again for the lighter on the bedside table when the woman said, "Can I have a cigarette?"

"Of course," Hanna replied and placed one in her mouth.

In so doing he levered himself up, so that they were no longer belly to belly, but side by side. The woman stretched herself. Hanna lit first her cigarette and then his own with the lighter. He inhaled deeply for the first puff. When he spoke, his face was masked from the woman by the intervening smoke.

"Do I talk in my sleep?"

"A little."

"Do I really? What do I say?"

"Not much in words. You seemed to be very upset about something."

"What words did I say?"

Hanna blew gently into the smoke, which was dispersed so that he could see the woman's face.

"Words like *avancez* and *on les aura*. That was all. I didn't know you'd been a soldier."

"No, I haven't been a soldier."

"But you'll have to do your military service if you become a French citizen."

"Yes," Hanna said. "In this century it seems impossible for a man to avoid becoming a soldier."

"Your dream made it sound as though you had been a soldier."

"I must have been dreaming about a war film," Hanna said. "I went to the cinema earlier this week."

"What film did you see? I adore war films. I like all films, but war films most of all. You see, my evenings are never free so I go to the matinées to amuse myself."

"I understand," Hanna said. "I've forgotten the name of the film. No, wait a second, it was *Taxi to Tobruk*."

"Oh, that," the woman said. "I've seen that too. It's too sentimental for me. Did you see *Escadrille Lorraine* or *Le Sergent X*?"

"No," Hanna said. "I don't like war films very much."

"I do," the woman said. "Films are either about sex or war and I get enough sex in my job and war makes a change."

"I prefer drinking as a relaxation," Hanna said.

"Good: let us drink to the future."

"No, let us drink to the present."

After a little more drinking tears began to pour down Hanna's cheeks; he tried to stifle them, but they flowed on unchecked. Finally he began to sob and stifle aloud. Then the woman, who had been drinking seriously throughout, took notice.

"Are you thinking of *her*?"

"No," Hanna sobbed. "I was thinking of my mother. I haven't written to her since I came back to Paris and that's six weeks ago. She will think that I never remembered her."

"I haven't written to my mother for ten years," the woman said. "She wasn't able to read the letters when I did write. That's why I stopped writing. I didn't want the neighbors gossiping about me."

"I owe everything to my mother," Hanna said.

"Are you an only child?"

"No, I have two brothers and two sisters, but I was closer to mother than any of them. Father never understood me. He wanted me to join the family business: insurance. Can you imagine me as an underwriter? Besides, my brothers were in it already. I wanted to be a pilot and mother paid for my flying lessons. It wasn't my fault that I was color blind—was it?— but the way my father talked you'd have thought it was. As though it mattered, not being able to tell blue from green. But I was a poet, too, and the only place to write poetry is Paris. Mother got me a job with an airline and paid my expenses when I got a transfer to Paris. I had to be in aviation, you understand? Even as a clerk. My head was full of Saint-Exupéry even though I could not experience his world."

"I am not religious," the woman said.

"I wasn't talking of religion," Hanna said.

"This saint you mentioned, the one who gave you visions, made me think you were religious," the woman said.

"He was a writer," Hanna said, "and a philosopher."

"Like Saint François de Sales?"

"No, he was a modern philosopher: he wrote about flying: Antoine de Saint-Exupéry."

"Oh, well," the woman said, "I still don't see anything to

cry about unless she's going to cut off your allowance."

"My mother doesn't make me an allowance," Hanna said. "She just sends me money from time to time."

"Well then, you can just play the prodigal son the next time you see her. And the longer you leave it the better."

"It will be a lifetime," Hanna said. "But a life cannot be counted in time, can it?"

"I don't know," the woman said. "What else is there to count it by? You talk about life in general terms—I remember I've had to listen to this sort of thing all night from seminarians on the loose just when I wanted to go to sleep—but I don't think it exists as a separate thing. There is my life and there is your life and there is General de Gaulle's life: but it's individual life. It only exists as we see it. Life is only the impression it makes on each of us as individuals. There is no separate life unless there is a God and then he sees it. But for human beings there is only the life of the individual and that's all mixed up with hope or else we wouldn't want to live it and the hopes are as real as anything that happens to us. I know this because I've really lived, I've lived hard, and you haven't, you've just read books and concocted theories. Life is as you see it and it doesn't matter whether you see it as a studio or a laboratory, it's only what you see, not what the man with the photographs or the girl in the next doorway sees. I know."

"Yes," Hanna said, "I suppose you are right. You must be right: there is no argument that can disprove what you say. But if you had, say, only one day of life to live, how would you spend it?"

"I'd do something I liked doing," the woman said. "I might take a bottle of marc and go and see a war film or I might go into the country, to an inn I know at Moret-sur-Loire, and I'd eat the best meal of my life, and I'd smoke English cigarettes and I'd drink nothing but whisky, real English whisky, and I'd get pissed as a Pole and know it wouldn't matter because I wouldn't have to wake up to a hangover, not that I ever get hangovers, but when I do get a hangover it's a bad one, about four o'clock in the morning, and I think about all the things I might have done if I'd been different, and then I have to get up and drink Casanis until I'm pissed again because you can't get a hangover twice running, only a sort of dreamy feeling, which I suppose is like being dead or dying."

"But supposing you were involved with someone?" Hanna asked. "Wouldn't you want that person to know how you were going to meet your death? Would you choose to die anonymously, as most people have died in wars in this century, or would you try to do something that someone would remember you by?"

The woman said nothing for several minutes: when Hanna had finished speaking, she took her left hand from the bottle and placed it beneath her left breast: the nipple was sprouting goose-pimples between the black hair; she drank from the bottle and then released the tit to pass her left forearm across her brow; then she clasped the breast again: it was still pimpled with chill. She looked at the chair and at the window and at the door. She took another drink from the bottle of marc: it was now two-thirds empty.

"Can I have a cigarette?" she said.

"Is that all you can say?"

"Give me a cigarette; I can think better when I'm smoking."

Hanna leaned over to the bedside table: in so doing he had to turn away from the woman: the back of his head was matted white: the woman touched it with her fingers, and Hanna turned, still holding the pack of Celtiques.

"What have you been doing?" the woman asked.

"What do you mean?"

"The back of your head is all white."

"Is it?"

"And the pillow is dirty."

"Is it? I must have been lying against the wall. I'm a very restless sleeper. Cigarette?"

The pillow was separated from the wall by the iron grille of the bedstead.

They both lit up and lay on their backs smoking and blowing the smoke toward the ceiling, which was peeling with the eczema of age and neglect. Presently Hanna began to blow smoke rings: he created three perfect rings that rose like halos and dissolved like ectoplasm.

"Tell me," the woman said and stopped speaking.

"What?"

"Tell me—oh, nothing. Tell me nothing. Promise you will tell me nothing. Promise me. Promise."

"I promise. I have told you nothing. Where do we go from here?"

"Let's pretend that this is the last day of our lives. We could have fun. Let's go out and eat. I'm starving. I'm so hungry that the marc is beginning to turn acid on my stomach. Let's eat."

"I don't want to go out," Hanna said. He blew another smoke ring, only this time it was not quite perfect, but wavering at the outer edges, and it was dispersed before it entered the cobweb-and-plaster world above them. He lit another cigarette from the butt of the first before remembering to offer the pack to the woman, but her cigarette was only half consumed and she refused.

"We could stay here and eat," the woman said. "Sozanski, if that is his name, often brings meals up from the Ali Baba. Just mutton and *cous-cous*, but they do it well. It's a little fat, but not tough. Only the shank-end is tough. You have good teeth. I'm really hungry or I wouldn't suggest it. Do you realize it's after three o'clock? He won't overcharge us for it because that cow of a *patronne* will be out shopping. If you pay me for the meal I'll buy a liter of wine. I wouldn't ask you if I wasn't so hungry that it makes my head go round and I imagine all kinds of things and I can't think properly. I'll pay for the meal. If I just ring the bell, Sozanski will come up with a tray. It will be all right. I'll pay for the meal as well as the wine. If I ring the bell Sozanski will come."

"I don't want anyone to come," Hanna said.

"I'm hungry," the woman said. "I can't think properly because I'm so hungry and I've had so much to drink."

"*Ça y est,*" Hanna said. "All right." He rang the bell. Nothing happened. He rang again. No one came.

"He must have gone back to the Ali Baba," the woman said. "I'll go myself."

"I don't want you to leave me."

"Why not?"

"You might not come back."

"How will you know until you let me go?"

"Why should I trouble to find out?"

"Because then you will know whether you have an ally or whether you are alone."

"You're not stupid," Hanna said.

"No," the woman said. "A woman can be many things, but never stupid."

"Then go," he said.

The woman got out of bed and Hanna stubbed out his cigarette on the surface of the bedside table and lit another. The varnish scorched into a yellow scab. Hanna lit another cigarette. The woman smelled the scorching and turned around: she had on her sweater and was struggling into a girdle.

"Don't do that," she said. "The old cow will begin to moo-moo as though it's milking time when she sees the mess. And she'll make me pay for the damage."

"She'll probably have other things to think about," Hanna replied. He flicked some ash onto the floor.

"Christ," the woman said. "I've got to live and work here."

"Take some money," he said. He drew down the corners of his mouth; suddenly he was much older and very tired. "You'll need some money for the food anyway."

"Can I get a bottle of Casanis, too? We could drink it with lots of water and it would be thirst-quenching."

"Do what you like."

"Can I have two thousand five hundred? It won't be more, I promise you."

"Take what you like," Hanna said. "Take it all. I won't be needing it."

The woman was drawing on her stockings: she paused with one leg in mid-air and almost overbalanced. She had to place one foot on the bed to avoid falling. Her lower lip hung down: it was glistening.

"Do you mean that? Is it here?"

"Don't touch that!" Hanna shouted as her hand fell on the briefcase. He caught the woman by the pubic hair and tugged until she screamed and dropped the case on the chair.

"Beast," she said. "There was no need to do that." There were tears in her eyes.

"Don't touch that case."

"All right. Tell me where the money is."

"Bring me my wallet. In case you need to know, it's in the breast pocket of my jacket. You're not so innocent that you don't know where a man keeps his wallet."

"Let me put my pants on first."

The woman stepped into her briefs, which had once been white but were now ocher about the gusset, and then took the wallet from the jacket and approached the bed. She was watching Hanna's right hand.

Hanna gave her a note for fifty New Francs: his wallet was full of tens and fifties: he let her see the notes before closing it and putting it beneath the pillow.

"You'll get the rest when you come back with the *couscous*. Do you understand? Now get out."

The woman put on her skirt, shuffled into her shoes, and went out. The door slammed behind her. He heard her exclaim when she reached the stairs; someone was cleaning them with a great clatter of brush and dustpan. The woman struck up a conversation with the other, evidently the *patronne*. They were talking about the mess on the stairs and about the shooting. The *patronne* told the woman that her husband was still drinking in the Ali Baba under the pretext of helping the police, when he should have been clearing up the mess. She had tried to drag him back to his duties, but the major—a real character!—had sent her away. One could not quarrel with the police, one had one's living to think about, but one could quarrel with dissolute husbands who sat drinking Casanis while their wives were insulted: the quarrel was a pleasure to come. She was going to have a word with him just as soon as he had finished hobnobbing with the *flics*. Presently the voices died away in a flurry of excuses and then the clatter of cleaning ceased also and there was silence. Hanna lay on the bed smoking and blowing a series of perfect, or nearly perfect, smoke rings at the ceiling. Occasionally a smoke ring was ruined by a suppressed sob.

Presently he heard footsteps on the stairs: they were the footsteps of a man. There was a knock on the door.

"Come in, major," Hanna said. His lips barely moved. He looked neither up nor around when the door opened. It was as though he had lost the power to move.

"I never reached the rank of major," the man who had come into the room said. "But if you insist on a rank I am Captain Sozanski and I have brought you your lunch." The man bowed slightly and stiffly from the waist and placed a plate of *cous-cous*, steaming and savory, and a great chunk of bread on the bedside table. It was the military man whom Hanna had seen go into the Café-Restaurant Ali Baba that morning.

"I'm not hungry," Hanna told him.

"Nevertheless I advise you to eat. You will feel better when you have eaten. I am an older soldier than you: take my advice."

"What makes you think I am a soldier?"

"*Fellagha* then, or militant, if you prefer it: it comes to the same thing. I wouldn't be here if I thought you were a common murderer."

"You've come from the police, haven't you?"

"Yes, and I have much to say to you and very little time in which to say it because the woman will soon be back." Sozanski walked stiffly across the room to the window that looked down upon the Ali Baba. "But first I want you to get dressed and eat. A man cannot fight really well with his belly empty or with his ass bare: it destroys his self-respect." Sozanski spoke in a mixture of formal phrases and argot, like a child in the playground after a reading lesson.

"What makes you think I'm going to fight?" Hanna asked.

"Would you rather be handed over to the *harkis* after killing one of them? If you surrender now you won't live to stand trial, I assure you."

Hanna stubbed out his cigarette on the tabletop and began to pull his trousers over bare limbs. Without turning around Sozanski said, "Get properly dressed: this is the last opportunity you'll have."

Some quality of command in Sozanski's voice seemed to galvanize Hanna: he was fully dressed within five minutes; then he took up the fork and plunged it into the *cous-cous.*

"That's better," Sozanski said. "That's a lot better. Good for morale. Do you mind if I have a drink? That looks like a rather passable bottle of marc."

"Help yourself," Hanna said and gestured to the flask with his fork. His mouth was full of mutton.

Sozanski filled the cup of the flask and drained it in one swallow. Then he took the cup to the sink and rinsed it thoroughly before screwing it back on the flask. Hanna paused, his fork piled with *cous-cous.*

"Tuberculosis?"

"No, silicosis. I was a miner before I was a soldier. That's how I came to France."

"Don't worry," Hanna said, going on with his meal. "I don't think I'll live to die of disease."

"You have just a chance if you act promptly. That is why I want you to eat and regain your strength while you listen to what I have to say."

"Why should you help me?"

"Because I have betrayed you. Unwittingly. You see, I saw the *harki* after you shot him but before he returned your fire, and I knew he was aiming at the door, not at the crowd. Out of vanity, and over several glasses of Casanis, I convinced the major that mine was the correct version of what had taken place. When he called for the hotel register and saw your name, and recalled that you had been involved with the Algerians in the seventeenth of October manifestation, he knew that you must be the assassin. I'm sorry."

"I was a fool to register in my own name. How was I to know that the same officer would take charge of this case? Or that Kacemi would live so long after being shot?"

"Or that I would see him take aim and sing to the *flics*," Sozanski said.

"What have you got to reproach yourself with? You only did your duty as a citizen."

"Is it a citizen's duty to help the police at the present time? I doubt it. Anyway, it occurred to me during the conversation that the men I was now aiding bore an uncommon resemblance to the men I was outwitting twenty years ago."

"The Gestapo?"

"And the Milice. The Gestapo were foreigners with limited contacts, but the French police could make things very hard for an agent who had been dropped to sabotage production in the coalfields of Lorraine. I remember that in 'forty-three, when I was in Metz, the *flics* had me in a very similar situation to your own."

"Perhaps you had better explain my situation to me, since you know so much."

"Certainly. The major is convinced that you are the man, but since you are known to be armed and have already killed one *flic* they would prefer to take you by trickery, without a fight. It would be bad for morale, you understand, if you were to hold out for several hours and perhaps kill another *flic* or two in the process."

"They could have taken me for the asking when you came in," Hanna said. "How do they propose to arrest me?"

"The woman will bring you doped coffee. When you're asleep she will, if possible, remove your pistol and signal to the police when it is safe to enter."

"The bitch."

Hanna was mopping up the gravy on his plate with the remains of the bread.

"Don't blame her," Sozanski said. "She is under great pressure. She may not carry out the full program, but she will bring you the coffee. She has to do that. She has her livelihood to think of and that depends on police cooperation."

"Why did they allow you to come here?"

"They trust me. They believe I will do anything for alcohol and they are almost right. I have been sent to keep you quiet while they obtain a suitable drug."

"And what do you suggest I should do? Pretend to be drugged and then shoot my way out when the *flics* come to arrest me?"

"No," Sozanski said. "That is the sort of thing that can only be done in books. I doubt if you could deceive the woman even if you could get rid of the coffee. And they have two men on the landing above, ready to shoot you in the back if you attempt to go down the stairs. But if you do as I did in Metz in 'forty-three you may get away. At least you'll have a fighting chance."

"What did you do?"

"I was in a room, very much like this one, on the second floor with two windows. I opened one window and fired and attracted a few bullets: for you it will be simple because one window is already open. Then I wrapped my overcoat around the bolster and showed it at the other window, partly concealed by the curtains. When the bullets went into the bolster I gave a terrible cry and allowed it to fall. Then I began to scream my head off as though mortally wounded. The police left the street and dashed up the stairs, so I jumped out of the window, shot a *flic* who had been slow in following the others upstairs, and got away in the crowd. Not all the crowd was sympathetic to the Milice, you understand? I had friends there. I doubt if a Chapelle crowd is sympathetic to the *flics* either: it will contain Algerians and Communists and perhaps friends of yours. In any case it takes a lot of courage to stop an armed assassin on the run."

"If I'm still able to run after jumping out of the window."

"Ah, there perhaps I had an advantage over you: I had

been trained in parachute jumping and knew how to fall. But you are a young man and it is only a matter of fifteen feet or so. Remember to give at the knees and roll if necessary. You could, of course, throw out the mattress and jump on that, but it would give the game away. Better take a chance on the pavement."

Hanna got up and looked down into the street from behind the curtains: there were no longer any police in the street apart from the routine *harki* sentries opposite the hotel, at the carrefour Goutte d'Or, and at the corner of the boulevard de la Chapelle.

"Why have they withdrawn the intervention police?"

"To give you a sense of security," Sozanski said. "There are plenty of them at the police stations and in *paniers-salades* in the boulevard de la Chapelle, but if you can get past the *harkis* you should be able to lose yourself beyond the cross-roads."

"I'd better wait until it's dark."

"Don't do anything of the sort. It's only four o'clock now and if you put off drinking the coffee for another hour they'll know you've seen through the trick. You'd be worse off than in daylight. Surprise is your only chance."

Hanna turned away from the window: his face was grey and glistening again, as it had been in bed that morning.

"It's no use," he told Sozanski. "I've haven't got that sort of nerve. I haven't got a head for heights. I couldn't jump out of the window if the hotel were on fire."

"Another glass of marc will cure that."

"No, it won't. I can feel the courage running out between my legs whenever I look down into the street."

"You've got to try it: it's your only chance."

"How I choose to die is my business."

"No, it isn't. If they take you they'll make you talk before they kill you. Everyone talks under torture, if it's done by experts, and the intervention police are experts. I know: I've been tortured by the Milice."

"I won't be taken that way," Hanna assured him. "I'll have

a few drinks and then I'll try and shoot my way down the stairs. If I don't succeed I'll be killed. They'll shoot and shoot until they're sure I'm dead and I won't be taken alive."

"You won't get through."

"Perhaps I don't want to get through. You talk about getting through: getting through to what? To be hunted again. I'm not an Algerian, I'm Lebanese. France was the country of my choice and now I've lost faith in France. If I escape I'll be hunted. I'll be hunted and caught. The Algerians won't be much help to me. They're a coarse, vulgar people and just now they think of nothing but politics as a way of freedom, but when they've won their freedom they'll only have the politics left. It's different for you: you're a Pole: you're used to working hard and fighting back. I'm Lebanese. We're like the Swiss or the Swedes. We haven't fought since we became a nation. We Maronites—Catholics of a sort you wouldn't recognize—were almost exterminated a century ago. And what did we do? We sent for the French. We were persecuted by the Mussulmans, the people I'm helping now, God knows why. I admire the French though I detest them for the way they're fighting this war: I feel nothing but contempt for Algerians unless they've evolved into passable imitations of Frenchmen. Algeria is the only Arab country which hasn't evolved a civilization: they had to wait for the French to provide one. But for all that, they deserve their freedom like anyone else and they don't deserve what the French are doing to keep them down. That's why I'm on their side. But I despise them. I was born in a civilized Arab country and one of the privileges of the civilized man is to choose the manner of his death: in bed, or by accident, or by suicide. Only barbarians expose themselves to hazard. That's why we didn't resist the Turks or the Druses: we knew that to resist them was to resemble them. We preferred to die, secure in our culture."

"Have you no pride in our trade?"

"Proud of being a soldier? How can one be proud of doing murder? I leave that to thugs like Algerians or Poles: they can behave like madmen and jump out of airplanes and windows and break their legs and be shot out of hand like horses so that they can call themselves heroes. I prefer to die like a civilized man: with dignity and acceptance."

Sozanski walked over to the bedside table and took up the flask. "Have a drink."

"You think you'll have me fighting drunk? You won't, you know. I'll drink myself insensible first."

"Have a drink."

This time Hanna accepted the flask while Sozanski drank from the bottle. When they had done, Sozanski said, "You must escape. Not just to make a token gesture: you must escape if you can."

"Why?"

"When the *harki* fired into the door he hit the mailbox. There was a parcel in it containing the pistol that was used to shoot him. It was addressed to Mademoiselle Nefissa Saddok. The police discovered the parcel torn open by bullets. I imagine that Mademoiselle Saddok will be here to collect it at seven o'clock—the time she usually calls for her mail."

"Oh, Jesus, Mary, and Joseph," Hanna said. "It can't be true."

"If it isn't true how do I know about it?"

"Why didn't you tell me before?"

"I didn't want to distress you until you had concentrated on your immediate situation."

"But if I'm killed I won't be able to warn her."

"If you are killed in the street your death will be seen by the crowd and that should be warning enough. That is why you must break out of this room."

"She has no right to expect this of me," Hanna said. He took another drink and began to pace up and down the room: his eyes were suffused with blood specks. "What right has she to demand this of me? We are nothing to one another."

"You are demanding this of yourself," Sozanski told him.

"She has no claim on me," Hanna said.

"You have a claim on her," Sozanski said. "You're not fighting for love of the FLN."

"She is a Mussulman."

"I don't think theology enters into it," Sozanski said and turned away. He was smiling.

"She has knock-knees," Hanna shouted. "She has a face like anyone else's ass."

"Isn't this all rather pointless?" Sozanski asked. "You are either committed to this woman or you are not. It is not a question of choice: it is a question of decision."

"Why did you jump out of the window in Metz?"

"I loved my country."

"And you think I love this woman enough to jump out of this window for her?"

"Yes."

"The cow. She's never done a thing for me. The bitch. I hardly got beyond the tops of her stockings."

"So long as you get beyond the windowsill it will be enough."

Hanna stopped in mid-stride: his face was dashed with tears and salt: his breath rose in foul gusts.

"Oh, Christ," he said. "Have you no sympathy? I'm not afraid of death: I'm only afraid of dying in a terrifying way: my legs breaking like matchsticks: my skull split: crawling around in circles and shrieking. I saw men reduced to that on the seventeenth of October. Have you ever seen men like that, waiting to be killed?"

"It is better than lying in bed and saying, 'Come in, major.' "

"All right, I'm a coward. Every civilized man is a coward: cowardice is the cornerstone of civilization."

"The woman will be back soon."

"I don't want to leave this room."

"It is a refuge, not a sanctuary."

"I could take the woman as a hostage and go through the police cordon with a gun in her back. Like they do in America."

"Do you think the *flics* prize her life above your death?"

"I could take you as a hostage."

"Willingly."

"You're one of the brave bastards. And I suppose they'd still shoot me?"

"Even if you could take the major himself as a hostage, his men would shoot. He's not very popular."

"There is no argument by which I can be persuaded to break out of this room," Hanna said. "I've given my life for her; that's enough."

"You are arguing against reality," Sozanski told him. "Either you will die for this girl or you will live for her. The outcome may be different, but the way is the same. You are very fortunate to have found such a woman: I am twice your age and I have never found a woman for whom I would have undergone such a risk. That is my loss and your gain. Make the most of your opportunities. Good luck. *Merde.*"

And then Hanna was quite alone. He began to walk around the room, his fingers questing over the table and the mantelpiece for something to pick up. Then he saw himself in the scrofulous mirror above the washbasin. He soaped his face and hands with great care, dried them, combed his hair, and cleaned the comb beneath the tap before putting it back in its case, and then pushed the ends of his Boul' Mich' cravat beneath the points of his collar.

He was like this when the woman came back into the room bearing a tray with another dish of *cous-cous*, bread, and two cups of coffee.

"You forgot the wine—or was it Casanis?" Hanna said.

"Oh, my memory," the woman said. "I've had too much to drink."

"What kept you so long?"

"I was waiting for them to make a fresh *cous-cous* and the coffee. Didn't Sozanski tell you? I asked him to bring your meal so that you wouldn't be bored."

"I'm not easily bored."

The woman sat on the bed and began to eat as though she would never eat again, using fork and bread alternately to take the food to her mouth, with so much concentration that

Hanna stood and stared down at her. When the plate shone she looked up: her eyes were shining also.

"I feel better now," she said. "I feel much better."

"Do you?"

"I'm going to drink my coffee now. Do you want yours?"

"I'll have another marc first."

"Perhaps you're right. It isn't very good coffee, but I'll feel better for it."

The woman was drinking the coffee and smiling at Hanna and he was looking down at her, the right eyebrow raised so that he looked like a satyr, drinking marc from the cup of the flask, but the woman went on drinking the coffee and smiling up at him.

"Listen," she said. "I've been thinking about the money. You keep it. You've given me plenty and you're going to need it more than me."

"I was going to keep it anyway."

"Good," she said. "I'm glad."

"Have my coffee as well," Hanna said suddenly. "Would you like some marc in it? It'll taste better that way."

"No thank you," the woman said. "I've had enough."

"Take it."

But the woman was still smiling as her head lolled back and the cup fell to the floor. Hanna went down on his knees beside her.

"Nicole," he said. "What's the matter?"

"Nothing," the woman said. "Everything will be all right now. And my name isn't Nicole." She was lying flat on the bed now, her legs sprawling on the floor. She opened one eyelid, exerting all the muscular tension of a weight lifter. "My name isn't Nicole. Isn't it funny that you don't even know my name?"

"Christ," Hanna said. "I believe you drank it deliberately."

"Just put my feet up on the bed and put the coverlet over me so I won't catch cold," the woman said. It was like listening to a voice in another room. "That's it. It's the first time a man has got me to bed without getting in beside me." She began to yawn; when she began to yawn it was as though she would never stop. "I can't keep awake any longer. Thank you, Georges: it's been a lovely day: goodbye and good luck."

The woman's mouth fell open: soon she was snoring. Hanna began a feverish activity. First he drained the last of the marc from the flask. Then he drank the cold coffee. He took his pistol from the briefcase and slipped it in the right-hand pocket of his jacket. He pulled the bolster from beneath the head of the sleeping woman and recovered his wallet. He did this tenderly, supporting her head with his left hand while he pulled with his right, and then rearranged both pillows to support her. Smiling down at the woman, Hanna took four fifty-franc notes and pushed them into her brassiere; he kissed her on the forehead; the woman did not move. He buttoned the bolster into his trenchcoat and propped it against the bed. He went back to the briefcase and took out a spare clip of ammunition and put that in the same pocket as the pistol. He took the pistol out of his jacket pocket and put it into his trousers pocket. Then he did several knee bends, flexing and rocking; the pistol fell out. He took the ammunition clip out of the right-hand jacket pocket and placed it in the left. He put the pistol back in the jacket pocket. Then he took it out again and flicked off the safety catch. He put the pistol back into the jacket pocket. When he looked up light was fading.

There was a noise of a heavy vehicle grinding up the rue Fleury in low gear. Hanna ran to the window and flattened his back to the wall. A *panier-salade* with armored shutters over the windows was reversing up the street. It stopped just short of the entrance to the Hôtel de l'Univers et de la Chapelle with a convulsion of the clutch. A voice spoke, booming yet muffled: as though the major were speaking through a megaphone from the front seat.

"Are you there, Hanna? If you can hear me, throw your pistol down into the street. Come out and give yourself up to French justice. The area is surrounded. You cannot escape."

Hanna began to shiver: he looked enviously at the bolster that wore his trenchcoat.

"We know you're there, Hanna," the voice boomed again. "Come out with your hands clasped behind your head. But first throw your pistol into the street."

Hanna could see the *harki* sentinel across the street, sunk deep in his doorway, submachine gun at the ready. As the seconds passed, the *harki* began to move forward by centimeters. Hanna drew the MAB 35 and found he could cover the *harki* from behind the fold of the curtain at the open window. He lowered the pistol.

"Come out, Hanna," the voice boomed. "Surrender or we will open fire. I will give you ten seconds. Counting: ten, nine, eight, seven . . ."

Hanna had the *harki* in his sights again. He said aloud, "Oh, well, it's war and he's the enemy."

". . . four, three, two . . ." boomed the voice.

At the count of "zero," Hanna fired twice at the *harki* in the doorway: one bullet ricocheted off the wall, the other smashed the shop window. The *harki* jumped back into the shop and then put a burst of fire into the Hôtel de l'Univers et de la Chapelle from behind the counter. The awning of the shop front spoiled his deflection and the bullets spent themselves in the flaking stucco, raising a powder storm that drifted through the open window and made Hanna cough.

The woman on the bed slept.

Hanna spat out the dust and moved to the other window, overlooking the crossroads. The second *harki* came forward at a crouching run, gun at shoulder. A crowd of passers-by had gathered, grouping themselves at the corners in a sort of fearful curiosity. Hanna lifted the dummy: he ruffled the curtains, but kept his head against the wall. The *harki* was looking down the street at the open window. Still holding the dummy, Hanna covered him with the MAB 35; but onlookers kept passing before his sights. He lifted the weapon and smashed a pane with the muzzle. The *harki* reacted at once: a burst tore the dummy from Hanna's left hand and flung it across the room; bullets tore great splinters from the window frame. Hanna gave a cry from the diaphragm that was all fear; then he began a series of simulated screams, falsetto, but very loud. The *harki* from the crossroads was smiling and reloading. The *harki* opposite had come from behind the counter and was again standing in the shop doorway. Hanna went on screaming. His voice was becoming hoarse, agonized. The rear door of the *panier-salade* was opened from within and a score of intervention police ran for the door of the Hôtel de l'Univers et de la Chapelle. They were equipped like soldiers: steel helmets of the pattern worn by poilus in the First World War; MAT 49s; bulging ammunition pouches. The major and the handsome young sergeant came after them. Hanna could hear the uproar they were making in the hall below. He went on screaming.

The screams above and the confusion below lasted several minutes. Finally the two *harkis* came to the hotel entrance. Hanna could hear the voice of the major. He heard the words "trick" and "send for tear gas." And still he went on screaming.

The woman on the bed was snoring but her snores were inaudible.

The crowd was much closer now that the sentinels were gone. A burly character in blue dungarees and a railwayman's peaked cap had formed a circle. Suddenly he cupped hands and bawled, "Come on, you *flics*. Are you afraid of one wounded man? The odds are a hundred to one. Isn't that enough for you? Or do you need the FTP to help you out?"

At the end of each sentence the crowd cheered the railwayman and booed the *flics*: the Francs-Tireurs et Partisans had been a Communist resistance group with an active cell in the eighteenth *arrondissement* during Occupation.

Another man in the crowd began to cry, "*Au secours les flics! Les flics sont emmerdés.*" The people took up the cry.

Hanna heard a man coming up the stairs: the man appeared to be trying to combine haste with stealth and was achieving neither. Hanna sat down on the sill of the open window. He looked down into the street and swayed and raised his eyes to the rooftops. A man in the crowd cried,

"*Voilà l'assassin!*" The big railwayman clapped a hand over his mouth. Another man took up the cry of "*Les flics sont emmerdés*" in a deafening voice: the voice of Sozanski.

"It seems that I have friends down there," Hanna told himself aloud. "Now jump."

He closed his eyes and raised a leg to the sill.

The door of the room burst open and a man lay sprawling on the floor: an automatic pistol clattered to the farther wall. Hanna had forgotten to lock the door after the woman returned and the catch had given at the first pressure. The man on the floor was the handsome sergeant: he had come through the door with the point of one broad shoulder, and meeting so little resistance to his charge, had been caught off balance. He was winded and disarmed: a killer fish whose very strength and ferocity had led it to swallow the baited hook.

Then he saw Hanna at the window and began to lever himself up.

Hanna put both feet back on the floor. He drew the MAB 35 and steadied himself with his left hand by holding the upper part of the window frame.

"Well, *flic*," Hanna said, "I might have guessed it would be you. So you rushed the door to become a hero at my expense. What does it feel like to find yourself at the feet of a *moujahidine?*"

"I am at a disadvantage," the sergeant said.

"You underestimate the gravity of your situation," Hanna told him. "Do you remember the man you shot in the boulevard Saint-Germain on the night of the seventeenth of October? Do you remember the girl who was searched?"

"*Raton*," the sergeant said. "I don't argue with little rats."

"Jump," someone shouted from the crowd below. It was the voice of the big railwayman. But Hanna had turned his back on the crowd.

"I may be a *raton*," Hanna said, "but I'm going to die fighting like a king rat. You're going to die like a snake: on your belly. You've been promoted since I last saw you and you have a piece of ribbon on your chest, but you'll still die as you've lived: a snake. Tell me frankly, what does it feel like for you, a man who has always held the gun, to be at the wrong end of the barrel? Will you die well?"

"Better than you," the sergeant said.

"We'll see," Hanna said.

"Jump," shouted someone in the street: it became a universal cry.

Hanna fired twice. The bullets hit the head of the sergeant at a range of not more than one meter: the first took him in the jaw and wiped out his fine profile; the second took him in the temple and bespattered the sleeping woman with fragments of bone and brain.

Then the upper half of the window came down across Hanna's thighs: his legs were trapped inside the room but his body was on the sill, back to the street. He smashed the pane with his left hand, lacerating his fingers to the bone as he gripped the centerpiece, which was studded with jagged glass, for support. Braced like this, he shot the first guardian of the peace to come up the stairs, so that the man fell back upon those below.

"Look out behind you," Sozanski shouted from the street.

Hanna, his left hand pumping blood into the street, shot a *harki* who darted out of the doorway of the hotel: the bullets blasted the forage cap from the auxiliary's cropped skull and threw him flat on his face in the gutter.

"Jump," the crowd was shouting. "Jump."

The magazine of the MAB 35 was empty. Hanna could not reach the clip in his left-hand pocket without letting go of the window frame with the hand that hosed the pavement with scarlet blood: he was swaying backward to the extremity of that arm.

"Listen," he shouted to the people below. "I have them bottled up: all the *flics*. If they come up the stairs I will shoot them and if they come out of the door I will shoot them. I have them trapped."

The crowd was still calling upon him to jump.

"Listen," Hanna bawled above their clamor. "You will see

how a free man can die when he is trapped. Remember that: I am a free man still, freer than any of you, although I am trapped. Tell Nefissa how I died. I may not have lived well, but by God, I am going to die well. Tell Nefissa how I died. Tell her how well I am dying."

Two *harkis*, sentinels on the other side of the block, came to the crossroads silently on their rubber-soled boots. They were among the crowd and aiming their guns at Hanna's back before anyone could cry a warning.

The *harkis* opened fire together before any man knew they were there. They fired first into the body and then began to make target practice with the extremities. They shot the MAB 35 out of his right hand. They fired into his left arm and he lost his grip on the frame. His body fell backward, though still pinned by the thighs. His wallet fell out of his breast pocket: its blood-stained contents fluttered over the crowd: money, a receipt for an application for French citizenship, a photograph of a swarthy girl. The back of Hanna's head hit the bullet-pitted stucco below the sill with a sound like a judge's hammer commanding attention. And the crowd was silent.

Hanna was hanging upside down, his empty hands dangling, and both were bleeding. His irises had rolled up under the lids; only the whites were visible. The heavy shoulder muscles held the arms outspread: he was like a man crucified upside down because he had judged himself unworthy to die upright.

The intervention police poured out of the hotel and began firing into the body. They went on shooting long after Hanna was dead.

interrogation

⊕   At that time of year and that hour of morning only clandestine lovers met in the Jardins du Luxembourg. A few couples were already abroad. It had been raining in the night, but the wind had risen with the day. Leaves fell like tears to obscure the artistry of the Marie de Médicis fountain. The cloak of Polyphemus was burdened by them; one of his eyes patched; his privy parts rendered truly private with the mock-modesty of Adam. A child's boat was tacking across the pool of the fountain; modeled on a Breton fishing trawler, it had red sails and a blue hull, haven-chipped. The wind now swelled the sails into opulent motion, now bore down so heavily that they were beaten to the water; so that only the buoyancy of a hull carved from the still-living wood enabled the boat to swim and saved her sails from saturation.

A girl was making the boat do battle with wind and water. She took gritty pebbles from the path and aimed them with such accuracy that their splashes made the toy sail before the wind until becalmed by a corner; then she would drive it forth, sending shot after shot beneath the stern, until it once more rode the embryo storm. The girl seemed to have no object other than to make the boat master the elements.

An old man was squelching across the spongy turf. From time to time he paused to impale sheets of *France-Soir* on a sharpened stick. He was muttering and the wind bore his words. He was telling the wind of lovers who concealed questing hands behind newsprint and cast it away when frozen fingers had lost all feeling.

As he spoke the old man was watching the desecration of the gravel path by the girl.

The old man stalked the girl until he was within speaking distance; but he did not speak. He was looking at the girl as a girl with a sort of sensual enjoyment that only an old man can find in a girl. He had ceased to speak of lovers. He was looking at the girl's legs, which were revealed to coltish length; for now she was leaning so far over the parapet that the old man could see above the tops of her stockings.

The stockings were black fishnet: it was like staring through leaded panes into a sanctuary.

Above and beyond her legs the girl was sheathed in black leather: coat and skirt seemed to creak with her movements. There was little that the imagination of a man, however old, could do to penetrate a figure so literally hidebound. Gradually the pleasure went out of the old man's face and was replaced by annoyance. Then he saw a discarded sheet of newspaper conveniently close behind her and bent low to pick it up, not looking down at the newspaper, but up at the girl's thighs.

And then the girl rounded on him. The old man was caught stooping: he tried to straighten himself, but age and infirmity were against him; his mouth fell open, but still he said nothing. The newspaper, also disturbed, fluttered at his feet.

The girl was as fascinating as a gargoyle: a claw face: hooded eyes, beak nose, hook chin. Her eyes held so much fire that the rest of her seemed charred by them: it was as though she were consuming herself, like a volcano.

"What are you doing?" she asked the old man.

"Me?" the old man said. He straightened himself a little. "Are you asking me what I'm doing here?"

"Are you deaf?"

"I am an official," the old man said. "It is my duty to be here."

The old man straightened himself a little more: he was now almost upright for his age: he raised a stiffened forefinger and pointed to his peaked cap.

"I can see that," the girl said. "I've got eyes. You didn't notice that I have eyes, did you? You only noticed that I have legs."

"Mademoiselle," the old man began, "I saw you . . ."

"Oh no you didn't," the girl contradicted him. "But that's what you were trying to do."

"Mademoiselle," the old man, a ramrod now, repeated, "it is forbidden to throw stones into the fountain."

The girl's face became a mixture of passion and compassion.

"Then we both have illicit pleasures," she told him.

"Mademoiselle . . ." the old man continued.

He stopped because a sea change had come over the girl's eyes: the lava had gone grey as pumice.

"Oh, go and masturbate," the girl said.

She picked up another handful of pebbles and turned her back on him.

"You are badly brought up," the old man shouted.

But the girl was already throwing stones into the pool; so the old man went grumbling across the grass. On his retreat the old man passed a slightly built Algerian walking along the path to the fountain. He was vividly dressed and greasily groomed, with a black mustache trimmed to an inverted V; the wind trimmed three remaining tufts of hair and brought tears to ocher-bound eyes that looked furtively at the old man as though out of habit rather than occasion. The Algerian might have been fifty years old.

"*Alors*," the old man said to the wind. "*Alors!*"

He turned to witness the encounter between the two Algerians.

The girl rounded on the man when he still appeared to be out of earshot.

"*Zut!*" the old man said. "That one has ears like radar." He thought this over and added, "Or perhaps she is a witch."

The girl raised both arms in what was rather a dramatic form of greeting; the man struck himself over the heart and hastened his pace. The old man could watch no more; he turned away.

"*Zut alors!*" he told the wind. "Would you believe it after the fuss she made? She's just a tart waiting to meet her pimp."

And the old man turned from the scene and went on sticking errant newsheets like a hunter riding down wild boar.

But the man was only saying to the girl, "Mademoiselle Nefissa Saddok, I suppose?"

"Yes," the girl said. "Who are you?"

"My code name is Salah," the man said.

"You certainly don't resemble Saladin," the girl said.

"The name was not of my choosing," the man called Salah said.

"Your modesty amazes me," Nefissa said.

The man was now so close to the girl that she held out her hand: gravel-gritty, nibble-nailed, but so well proportioned that it appeared to have been designed rather than conceived.

Salah ignored the hand and attempted to kiss the girl, not upon the cheeks, but upon the mouth. He found the heel of the shapely hand beneath his thickened nose; grit was forced into his nostrils and Salah snorted his pain; something nudged him painfully in the crotch, just hard enough to remind him of the vulnerability of his organs: he looked down and saw the kneecap strained white beneath the fishnet, poised to deliver a second reminder.

"Idiot," he said. "Triple idiot. We're supposed to be lovers."

"Don't try to profit by it," Nefissa said.

"The way you're behaving I'm more likely to be diminished by it."

The girl did not smile: her eyes were basilisk; but Salah refused to be petrified.

"We're supposed to be playing a part," he reminded her.

"I'm a militant, not an actress," she told him. "Anyway, I find the role unconvincing."

"You're in a fine mood."

"Tell me what I want to know."

"The *harki* is dead."

"What of my man—our man?"

"Still in the hotel as planned."

"Is that all you have to say?"

"The *harki* lived long enough to fire back: two were killed:

an old man and a boy: Mussulmans but not our people.
Others were wounded and taken by the *flics*. I don't know
how many."

"Hanna?"

"He is in the hotel as I told you. We"—Salah stressed
the pronoun ever so slightly—"don't know whether he was hit
or not. I think not. The *harkis* came and checked on everyone
in the hotel and seemed satisfied. They made no more arrests.
They appear to think that the people the *harki* shot were
responsible for his death. But the Goutte d'Or is sealed off.
There are police barricades everywhere."

"I must go to him."

"No," Salah said. "You must wait with me. You have been
calling for your mail every evening at seven, when you are
supposed to be returning from your lectures. If you were to
call earlier it would look suspicious. The *flics* should have
lifted their barricades by tonight: they don't like loitering in
the dark in that area: they leave that to *harkis*, like Mohammed Kacemi. So you must wait."

"Don't talk to me like that, you, you who are in no danger.
He may be wounded and waiting for me."

Salah looked at the girl: he was so small and slight that
some dissipation seemed to have flayed the flesh and laid bare
the bone; but his eyes lived on: brown and blood-flecked:
indescribably old. He gave the girl a look like a blow, and
found himself outbraved. He looked away into the pool where
the fishing boat was becalmed between squalls.

"We are like the boat," he told her. "We can do nothing
until there is a favorable wind."

"I can make the boat move without the wind," the girl
said.

She stooped and picked up a pebble from the path and set
the boat sailing with a single shot.

"But it is voyaging without purpose."

"It serves my purpose."

"Not mine, and whatever you may think of me I am speaking for the Special Organization."

"So the Organization has become becalmed like a fishing smack," the girl said. "I could make the Organization move."

She threw a pebble with such vicious accuracy that it actually clipped the stern of the boat and set the bows awash with sudden motion.

Salah said nothing for a long time: he was looking down at the pointed toes of his shoes; all the while the girl was watching the boat.

"I know that I'm in no immediate danger," Salah said at last. "That is because I'm so well known to the police for my other activities. I am also a police informer: I did this before I began to work for the Organization. Even when I am betrayed—and I have several times been betrayed—the police cannot believe it. They know that I am also a blackmailer and draw the obvious inference that the informer is one of my victims. I am too useful to the police. I am one of their links with the Mussulman underworld: they cannot believe that a man like me can also be a patriot."

"Are you?"

Salah struck the balustrade with the heel of his hand: the flesh went white: then blue: then red: it began to bleed; Salah seemed not to notice.

"No one else offered themselves for the job when I was elected," he said. "There is no one who wants to succeed me. Have you thought of the death the *flics* would give me if I were found out?"

"How could you be found out if you cannot be betrayed?"

"By one of the new men from the Ministry of the Interior: the *barbouzes*."

"You've been reading *Le Parisien libéré*," Nefissa said. "Either they don't exist or they're too busy tracking down their own traitors: the Secret Army Organization. You are inventing dangers, like a schoolboy, while you live on the courage of people like Hanna and myself. What dangers do you run as a courier? Where were you on the seventeenth of October?"

"I was in a police station," Salah shouted. "I was laying information about the march of a column to the pont Neuilly: information they already had, but it helped to establish confidence and gave me an alibi. That's what I did on the seventeenth of October. I obeyed orders and saw my countrymen bleed and the *flics* swagger. I did what I have always done, ever since the first of November, 1954: I obeyed orders, which is all I am asking you to do."

Salah sucked some of the bloody grit from his hand and spat into the pool: the spittle coagulated into an eddy, making its own separate peace with the troubled waters.

"Don't be filthy," Nefissa said. "You might foul the boat."

Salah bit a piece of frayed skin from his hand and spat it on the path.

"All I ask is that you trust my judgment," he told her. "Your life is my responsibility. So is Hanna's life. Do you think I'm not just as much concerned about Hanna as you are—in a military sense? Can't you trust me?"

"Who are you that I should trust you? A pimp?"

"I am a man who has been seven years at war," Salah said and he spat more fouled blood on the path. "Where were you on the first of November, 1954?"

"I was a schoolgirl in a smock," the girl said. "My parents had sent me to school in France the year before. When the war began the other girls began to notice that I was an Algerian. Some of them were the daughters of army officers who were fighting in Algeria. One of them called me a *raton* and slapped my face when we were in the showers. It was very strange because my parents are assimilated. My father is a civil servant in Algiers. I had never thought of myself as an Algerian until the girl slapped my face: I was a French Mussulman."

"I wonder if any of you youngsters will remember what it was like for us when the war is over?"

"What what was like?"

"What it was like for us veterans: the criminals: the people who had the contacts which got the Organization going. What shall I be able to say to my sons? That I carried orders and sent men and women to their deaths?"

"After that girl slapped my face," Nefissa said, "I became conscious of my destiny: I began to read Simone de Beauvoir."

"I've never been able to read much," Salah said. "That's one of the difficulties of speaking Arabic in the cradle and French in the street: I've never mastered either language. Perhaps that's why I began to deal in photographs."

"It's been a long war," Nefissa said. "Seven years long. I was a child when the war began. I've grown up with the war. I don't know what life would be like without the war."

"It's been a slow war," Salah said and spat again on the path: this time the blood was clean. "Today has quickened it. Today has shown the bastards that they can't get away with torture in Paris. We never thought Hanna would do in the *harki*. We didn't think he'd make a *moujahidine*."

"I made him a *moujahidine*," Nefissa said. "It was the price I put upon myself."

"I wouldn't do that for any woman."

"You are not Hanna."

"I'm glad I'm not Hanna."

"No one could ever be Hanna. He is a poet of action. He has done his part. All that remains is for us to save him."

"You have only to collect the parcel tonight" Salah explained. "That will remove the evidence. Tomorrow morning he will be able to walk out of the hotel and even if the *flics* tear the place apart there will be nothing against him."

"What shall I do with the parcel?"

"Go to Les Halles, rue Saint-Denis."

"I wouldn't go there at night by myself," Nefissa said. "What do you think I am? One of your whores?"

"That will be all right," Salah said. "You will be watched. No one will molest you. I have influence in the district."

"I don't doubt it."

"A man will accost you."

"I'm not surprised."

"It will be the right man. A big man who looks like a Frenchman. A big truck driver. He will say, 'I've come a long way to meet you, sweetheart.' "

"How flattering."

"You will reply, 'But you still have far to go.' Then you will take his arm and walk with him to a hotel which he will indicate and in the foyer you will pass the parcel to him and leave. I trust that handbag is large enough to take the parcel?"

"Of course. Hanna and I have already tried it."

"Good. That is all you need to know."

"Surely there are easier ways of getting rid of the pistol. Wouldn't it be easier to throw it into the Seine?"

"Yes, but good automatic pistols are expensive and this one has been serviced by experts."

"It is evidence against Hanna," Nefissa said.

"Only so long as it is in the hotel," Salah argued. "Once it is out of the hotel the ballistics experts might identify it as the weapon that killed Kacemi, but that is all. It won't carry Hanna's fingerprints: he was wearing gloves. It is only a danger to the man who uses it again. By removing the weapon you will have taken away all possible evidence against Hanna because his own pistol could not possibly have been used to kill Kacemi. That is why timing is so important."

"All right," Nefissa said. Suddenly she sounded tired. "What must I do?"

"You must remain with me until the time comes to go."

"Why?"

"Those are my instructions: they are for your own good. You might do something impulsive or you might have an accident, and then I would have to arrange something else."

"Do you mean that I must spend the day in your company?"

"Don't put it like that," Salah protested. "Let's go and have a coffee. It's cold standing here."

The girl said nothing, but went down the steps to the edge

of the pool, drove the boat inshore with two precise shots, and picked it out of the water. She dried the hull off with her handkerchief, lowered the masts, furled the sails, bound them with the rigging, and placed the boat beneath her arm.

"Let's go," she said.

"Aren't you going to leave it for the child?" Salah asked.

"There is no child," Nefissa told him. "It's my boat."

She led the way along one of the conjunction of paths: it led to the Boul' Mich'; Salah followed her, sucking his hand.

And so they walked in file through the Jardins du Luxembourg, past the soaked benches, the damp lovers, the blowing leaves that clung like limpets, and the sticky litter of children.

Nefissa turned left down the Boul' Mich'; the pavements were now achatter with students and typists; the roadway blocked with incoming traffic from the Porte d'Orléans; and a *flic* with an early-duty face was standing at the intersection of the rue des Écoles and letting it jostle for priority. They skirted the trees already fringed with motor scooters and bicycles, and went down past the great blocks designed by Haussmann so that artillery would have a clear field of fire against the mob, and the cafés that advertised English "breckfasts" ("Pork with eggs; steack at chips; jam; thea; sauce."), and the cinemas showing American Westerns until Nefissa turned left into the rue Hautefeuille and they came to the place Saint-André-des-Arts.

"Now we are in France again," Nefissa said.

They were standing before a taxidermist's window: it was filled with the skeletons of deer and dogs; a wild boar, stuffed and mounted; the heads of wolves and lions and, as a centerpiece, that of a full-grown elephant.

Salah was looking in at this display when Nefissa spoke.

"So I see," he said. "It is strange that the French cannot resist hunting things. They have killed all the beasts in their territories, so now they have taken to hunting men."

"Not that," Nefissa said. "I mean this."

She lifted her hands to the rioting rooftops, precarious balconies, yellow-washed walls, striped awnings, and vases of wilting flowers in memory of those who had fallen the last time war had come to Paris.

"Very pretty," Salah said.

"It is more Provençal than Parisian," Nefissa said. "Don't you feel the sunshine?"

"I only feel the cold," Salah told her, "and I could do with a coffee."

"Where are you going to take me?" she asked.

There were four cafés in the place Saint-André-des-Arts.

"That one," said Salah, pointing to the Café-Tabac Saint-André-des-Arts.

"Not me," Nefissa said. "I'm not going into that hole. Did you know that the manager refused Hanna admission on the seventeenth of October?"

"I know," Salah said. "But it will cost us nothing and that is important. Every franc saved is a franc spent on the war."

"I don't want their conscience money."

"It isn't conscience money. It is money they pay us for refusing Hanna. They contribute as reparation for refusing Hanna. The manager has become one of our star contributors in the district. He has had to stop juggling the books in his interest and juggle them in ours. One day he will make a mistake and the authorities will find out. Then he'll really be done for."

"Good!" Nefissa said. "Let's go and hasten his ruin."

An old man in a cloth cap so greasy that it glistened, his jaws distorted to clamp a pipe with his remaining teeth, was setting out marble-topped tables and cane-backed chairs on the terrace; but the cold drove them to the glazed terrace. The snot-nosed manager was remonstrating with several little Vietnamese students who were kicking a Gottlieb pinball machine in protest against the "tilt" sign; some glassy-eyed girls were dunking croissants in their coffee; a group of Algerian municipal workmen in blue overalls were swaying over their beer at the bar; the atmosphere was raucous with Edith

Piaf's "Rien," which someone had selected on the jukebox.

The manager saw the two Algerians and lost interest in the Vietnamese, who went back to kicking the Gottlieb with their little pointed feet until the coins rang; the manager passed the sleeve of his cardigan across his nose and waved away a waiter who had come to serve Nefissa and Salah; his face was contorted as though he were smiling.

"Good morning, m'sieu, 'dame," he greeted them.

"I am mademoiselle," Nefissa said. "You should be more observant." She set her boat down carefully on the table.

"Good morning, monsieur, good morning, mademoiselle," the manager said. "May I serve you?" He was still smiling.

"Or perhaps your eyesight is failing," Nefissa went on, "and you hadn't noticed that we are Algerian Mussulmans."

"That makes no difference to me," the manager assured them. "Half my customers are North Africans, as you can see for yourselves."

He pointed to the drunken workmen at the bar.

"Perhaps your memory is failing also," Nefissa said. "How many Arabs did you serve on the seventeenth of October?"

"That was different," the manager said. "There was a manifestation."

He could no longer smile.

"There was a manifestation on your part too," Nefissa told him. "A most unpleasant manifestation. You locked your doors against Mussulmans and even against a Christian Arab who had taken no part in the fighting."

"Listen, mademoiselle," the manager said, "I'm sorry about your friend, but I'm not interested in politics. I just want to be left in peace to run this business. I'm already paying for the seventeenth of October. Paying, you understand. Ask him." He gestured with a snot-stained arm at Salah.

"Don't point at me," Salah said. "It's rude."

"There is so much glass in this place," Nefissa said. "So many windows and so many mirrors. A bomb or a burst of automatic fire would cause a lot of casualties."

Salah said nothing: he was smiling and drumming on the table top with gloved fingers.

"Listen, mademoiselle," the manager said. "Almost half my customers are Mussulmans. I value their custom. I haven't turned away a North African since the seventeenth of October. This place is always filled with them."

"I wonder he doesn't fear for his safety," Nefissa said to Salah. "A *harki* was killed with a poisoned thorn the other day and the assassin went undetected."

The manager passed the sleeve of his cardigan across his nose and then across his forehead.

"Can't you stop her?" he said to Salah. "I'm paying. There is no reason why I should be insulted."

"Some of the militants are very bitter against you," Salah said. "It's very difficult to keep them in check. You should pay more."

Salah smiled: he had a double set of stainless steel teeth.

"I pay the FLN everything they ask," the manager said, leaning forward and speaking in a whisper. "I do that so that I can be left in peace to run the business. I don't want any trouble."

"I believe that," Nefissa said, still speaking as though to Salah. "It's probably the first true thing he's said in his life. But he's going to have plenty of trouble if he isn't careful because every time I see him I'm going to tell him what a dirty bugger he is."

"I don't want a fight," the manager said.

"You shouldn't provoke her," Salah said.

"I have not said anything to offend her," the manager said.

"You offend her by your presence," Salah said. "You'd better apologize."

"Me apologize?" the manager said. "Why should I apologize?"

"If he were to apologize to me I would spit in his face," Nefissa said to Salah.

"You heard that?" the manager said to Salah.

"I don't want to force the issue," Salah said. "Otherwise it might seem that your apology was not genuine."

Salah smiled his stainless smile.

"All right," the manager said. "All right, all right. Just tell me what I am to apologize for."

"I think you should apologize to this lady for the distress your presence causes her."

"I'm very sorry, mademoiselle, that my presence offends you," the manager said, bowing to Nefissa. "If you would be so kind as to give me your order I will take myself away. I hope you will accept my apology, mademoiselle."

"I hope I will be the one to kill you," Nefissa told him.

The echoes of the "Rien" died as she spoke and her words were very audible; two of the glassy-eyed girls got up and went twittering away.

The manager was looking at Nefissa with his mouth agape; his face had turned the same shade of soiled grey as his cardigan.

Salah said, "Bring us two *cafés crèmes* and two *croques-messieurs*," in his careful French.

"Certainly, monsieur," the manager said.

"And a pack of Gitane filters," Nefissa said.

"Of course, mademoiselle."

When the manager returned with the foam-topped coffee, the tiers of toasted ham and cheese, and the cigarettes, Nefissa said, "I'm not hungry"; then the manager was gone.

"Do you think I'm hungry?" Salah asked. "But I need food as you need food: we're both losing a lot of nervous energy. If I thought you would obey me I would order you to eat. As it is I can only set you an example."

And he bit deeply into the *croque-monsieur*, so that the grease glistened upon his stubbled chin. After a moment's hesitation, Nefissa began to slice her own *croque-monsieur* and then to eat it.

When they had done, Salah said, "We have the day before us: I suggest we go sightseeing. We shall be less conspicuous among tourists."

"We would be even less conspicuous among our own people and there are still some left, despite the deportations."

She opened the pack of Gitanes and offered it to Salah; he refused and took one of his own Celtiques before replying.

"We might be taken in for questioning if the *flics* decide upon a *ratissage*."

"Don't use that word," she said.

"You know what I mean."

"I know. Where shall we go?"

"To the zoo: we're quite close to the Jardin des Plantes."

"I can't bear to see anything caged," Nefissa said. "Especially today, thinking of him caged up in that hotel room."

"We could take a *bateau-mouche* from the Eiffel Tower," Salah suggested. "That's the best way to see Paris."

"I can never see enough of Paris," Nefissa said.

They left the Café-Tabac Saint-André-des-Arts without being given a bill.

Salah told the manager, "We'll be back presently."

"Guard the boat," Nefissa said, handing it to the manager. "Take great care of it."

"Whatever you say, monsieur, mademoiselle," the manager said: he cradled the boat with one arm and wiped his nose with the other.

"I wonder he doesn't go to the police," Nefissa said as they crossed the *place* to the bus stop at the bottom of the Boul' Mich'.

"He daren't do that because it would mean exposing his swindle to the management," Salah explained. "Then they might begin checking on his own private swindles. We have him."

Salah took numbered slips from the machine at the bus stop and by much shouting and jostling gained them their rightful priorities when the bus arrived. A trio of Tricolore flags marked the presence of some visiting celebrity and beside the cab was a poster urging them: "*Buvez Perrier—l'eau qui fait PSCHITT!*" It was a vintage vehicle with an open platform at the back and a bell like a lavatory chain. Salah would have pushed his way inside, but Nefissa detained him.

"Let's stay here," she urged. "The sight of those bubbles sloshing around in the Perrier bottles always makes me feel sick and we can smoke out here."

"OK," Salah said. He pronounced it "Oh-kah."

So they stood on the platform while Salah bought a ticket book and detached sufficient tickets for their journey and Nefissa lit another Gitane. Then they leaned over the rail, in defiance of the warning notices, and rubbed shoulders with the workmen who smoked Blue Gauloises and spat the resultant phlegm on the setts of the quai des Grands-Augustins.

"I think this is the best way to see Paris," Nefissa said.

The wind had parted her thick hair at the back and framed her narrow face: she looked like a vixen peering out of its earth: she was smiling.

The nape of her neck was darker than the rest of her skin and freckled: she smelled of soap and leather.

"I believe you love this city," he said.

"Oh, but I do. Do you find that strange?"

"Yes," he said. "I was born here."

"Loving Paris is like being in love with a person," Nefissa said. "It is not merely loving; it is acceptance: even the faults and the filth."

They got off at the pont Alexandre III and walked along the quai d'Orsay and the quai Branly to the landing stage of the *bateaux-mouches* below the Eiffel Tower. When they reached the stage, however, Nefissa halted.

"The water's too rough," she said. "It reminds me of the last time I came from Algiers to Marseilles. I would be sick."

"All right, we'll go up the Eiffel Tower instead."

"I have no head for heights."

"How do you cross the Mediterranean?"

"That's what I'm thinking of: it always makes me ill, either by sea or by air."

"Have you ever been up the Eiffel Tower?"

"No. I'd never get beyond the first stage. Well, let's go that far: it's too cold to hang around."

They stood in a line under the eyes of the Gendarmerie nationale, with their Sam Browne belts and modern automatic weapons. The gendarmes watched everyone: the Secret

Army Organization, Salah explained, was said to be plotting to seize the tower in order to broadcast from the emergency transmitter. The mobile gendarmes had replaced the Municipal Police because many of the latter, including their chief, Maurice Papon, were said to sympathize with the OAS. Most of the people in the line seemed indifferent to the gendarmes: they were provincials taking a winter holiday or servicemen on leave: it was late in the year for foreign tourists.

Salah bought tickets for the third stage despite Nefissa's protests. But she enjoyed the view from the first stage: she had never realized Paris could be so beautiful, she said. Fortified by coffee they went on to the second stage. Nefissa hesitated at the last elevator.

"I've never been to the top of the tower," Salah pleaded. "Isn't it strange that a Parisian like me should have to wait half a century before going up the tower? And I've met so many tourists here—often sold photographs to them at the foot of the tower. But this is the first time I've had a day to myself and money to see the sights."

Nefissa shrugged.

"After all," she reflected aloud, "I shall soon be taking a much greater risk than going to the top of a tower as thousands have done every day for years. The worst that can happen to me is that I shall be sick. Let's go."

Some parachutists entered the elevator at the last moment. They were all very young and noisy; all wore the ribbon of the Algerian War. They had cropped heads and shiny faces; the ribbons of their red berets dangled to their shaven napes. One of them, very fair and with very pale blue eyes, had a nervous tic of the jaw muscles: he twitched them continually; he was the noisiest of all.

"Is this a return ticket?" he asked the elevator man. "Or do we have to make our own way down?"

The paras thought this witty enough for an explosion of laughter; as soon as the French families noticed that the paras were rather drunk they began to gaze out of the windows.

Then the para with the tic noticed the two Algerians.

"This would make a good place for a *ratissage*," he told his comrades. "At least they'd have to stand and fight instead of scuttling off into the *bled*."

The paras thought this too very funny. Some of the fathers of families smiled; others frowned, but most pretended not to have heard.

The twitchy para removed his beret and bent his bullet head in a bow.

"Excuse me, monsieur, mademoiselle."

The paras were overcome with laughter; the families were overcome with interest in the ascending view.

Nefissa whispered to Salah, "If he is sober enough to notice that I'm not wearing a wedding ring he is drunk enough to be dangerous."

"Did you come provided with parachutes?" asked the twitchy para.

"The management gave us return tickets," Salah said. He laughed.

"I only asked because my comrades here, who are, I regret to say, drunk, are planning an entertainment which may make a sudden descent necessary."

The elevator stopped at the final stage and the French families got out, chattering briskly, going by groups, and not regarding their neighbors. Salah made a move to follow them, but the para with the tic prodded him in the chest so that he recoiled against the side of the cabin.

"Have you got your parachute?"

The other paras had formed a circle that sealed off the door.

"No, but I've got something better," Salah said and plunged his hand into his right pocket.

The twitchy para was at him before he could withdraw his hand; he had an armlock on Salah, the elbow bent back against the joint: Salah gasped and the other paras moved in closer.

"Now let's see what you've got," the twitchy para said.

The elevator man, who had frayed threads of ribbon running from the buttonhole of his jacket lapel, was looking the other way.

The para began to pluck Salah's imprisoned right hand from his pocket: Salah's shallow brow was awash with sweat: his close-set eyes were awash with tears. He grunted twice but was otherwise silent. His hand came away clasping a packet of postcards wrapped in a montage of views of Paris; his fingers fell apart and the packet dropped to the floor; the band burst and the postcards could be seen. The paras pounced on them with spontaneous hilarity.

"I thought you gentlemen might appreciate them," Salah said. "Please keep them as a souvenir of your visit. They're much more entertaining than anything you can buy in the shop here. I'm always glad to oblige our boys in uniform."

Nefissa tilted her head and tried to get past the twitchy para.

"Is this really you, mademoiselle?" he asked. "Forgive my asking such an intimate question, but the photograph does not really do justice to your . . . your face."

The other paras shouted their laughter.

Nefissa straightened herself so far as her stooped and narrow shoulders would allow; her face was chalk-livid: her eyes pumice grey.

"Gentlemen, soldiers of the French Army," she said, "would you make way for a soldier of the Algerian Army?"

The paras parted before her so that she went out upon the third stage of the Eiffel Tower as though between a guard of honor formed by the red berets.

"She's a real *fellagha*, that one," the twitchy para said. He threw down his card and looked at Salah, who was massaging his right elbow with his left hand.

"Pick that up, you dirty little man," the para said and followed Nefissa.

The other paras let their cards fall to the floor of the cabin and followed him out. They were commenting on Nefissa.

"Quel type ça."

"*C'est un gars gonflé.*"

"*Quel dur!*"

Salah was left alone among the litter: there was a press of people waiting to enter for the downward journey: a child stooped to pick up one of the cards: his mother slapped his hand and screamed.

"Clear up that mess before I send for the police," the elevator man ordered. "If I'd known what you were up to I wouldn't have allowed you in here. Trying to corrupt our boys in uniform . . . You should be ashamed of yourself."

By the time Salah had picked up all the cards, scrabbling for them with numb fingers, Nefissa had disappeared. He walked around the four sides of the tower and found her leaning against a window, eyes closed. Her mouth was pursed, the lips blue. Salah tried to get to her but one of the paras stopped him with an elbow in the ribs.

"What's the matter?" Salah asked. "What have you done to her?"

"She's fainting," the para said. "Shut up."

The para with the tic came from the bar carrying a miniature *ballon* of Courvoisier: he prised Nefissa's lips apart by pressing on the jaw muscles; then he poured the whole glass straight down her throat. Nefissa coughed; her eyelids fluttered; she flushed deep down below the black leather collar.

"She doesn't drink alcohol," Salah said. He tried to push through the paras.

"Shut up."

"She's not used to it."

"Shut up. Can't you see it's doing her good?"

"But she's a strict Mussulman."

"Go screw yourself."

The twitchy para brought a cup of black coffee and another glass of cognac; when he saw that Nefissa's eyes were open he tipped the cognac into the coffee before giving it to her.

"Drink this," he said. "Then you'll feel better."

"It's alcohol," she said. "I can smell it's alcohol; I feel as though I'm on fire."

"So it is," the twitchy para said. "It's done you good and we all do things we shouldn't do in wartime. It's one of the sacrifices you are making."

"Oh, I feel so strange," Nefissa said.

But she took the cup and began to sip the fiery, steaming mixture. Salah could not get near her; but when he saw that the paras meant Nefissa no harm he stopped trying to get past them. The paras appeared delighted with Nefissa: they kept saying how splendid it was to meet a real, live *fellagha*; they had never guessed that *fellaghas* could look like Nefissa or they would have held their fire and taken prisoners; they spoke grimly and behaved gaily. It was not clear whether they took Nefissa seriously but there was no doubting her popularity. They seemed to resent Salah.

When she was feeling better the twitchy para insisted on escorting Nefissa around the tower and showing her the best views; she leaned heavily upon his arm. Salah followed the group at a distance: he could not understand what was happening.

Presently she excused herself, saying she would go home and rest. The twitchy para thought she should see a doctor and offered to escort her; they would all escort her.

"No," she told them. "My uncle is with me and in times of sickness it is better to be with one's family."

"Is that your uncle?" the para asked, looking at Salah.

"Yes."

"Poor child. Do you want to go with him?"

"Yes, please. And thank you a thousand times for your kindness."

"*Au revoir, mademoiselle fellagha*," the para said. "When we meet again I hope it will not be in battle."

He kissed her on both cheeks. The other paras insisted on doing the same thing. They wished her "*bonne chance*" and "*merde*." She was quite breathless when she rejoined Salah at the lift.

Salah said nothing until they reached the ground.

"Where is your doctor?" he asked.

"I'm not ill," she said. "It was just vertigo: I told you I had no head for heights."

"Nor for brandy," he said, staring at the pointed toes of his crocodile-skin shoes.

"What has that got to do with you?"

"You're supposed to be in my charge," Salah said.

"And a fine job you made of looking after me."

"They were too many," he said.

"Not for me," Nefissa said.

"So I saw."

"Don't be silly: they were front-line soldiers, not *flics*."

"Have you never heard of the Villa Lodi in Algiers? That is run by paras."

"Not this sort of paras: they're just boys who were conscripted and thought it an adventure to volunteer for parachute training. Front-line soldiers only fight: it's the people behind them who do the harm."

"You intellectuals make me sick," Salah said.

"Fuck off."

"I must look after you until you collect that letter."

"How do you propose to go about it?"

"Would you like some lunch?"

"I've never felt less like eating in my life."

"Then let's go to the cinema. I know where there's a good Western."

"I don't like Westerns: the shooting gives me a headache and the sight of blood makes me sick."

"This one has Gary Cooper and Grace Kelly."

"Let's go," Nefissa said. "You've convinced me."

Salah, suddenly solicitious, insisted on taking a taxi to a cinema called the Ciné-Latin, near the Sorbonne, which was showing an American film dubbed *Le Train siffle trois fois*.

They left the cinema at five o'clock. Salah was humming "The Ballad of High Noon."

"Oh, La Kelly," Nefissa said. "How beautiful she is. Typically American, don't you think? And to think that she renounced her career to marry a poor prince."

"He's not so poor," Salah said. "He owns most of Monaco."

"Do you think I could ever get my hair like that?" Nefissa ran a hand over her head and pulled a strand down before her eyes; it was only just long enough. "It's so black and curly: I don't think that even Alexandre could get it beautifully blond and straight like hers, even if I let it grow."

"I like a good cowboy," Salah said. He pronounced it "coobwah." "I wish we had some marksmen like that on our side."

"We have Hanna: he got his man this morning."

"But that was only one man: did you see how Cooper killed three?"

"The last would have got him if it hadn't been for La Kelly."

"That was just put in for the sake of the women in the audience. I'll bet he could have got the lot by himself."

"Imbecile. Do you think he really killed those men? He probably doesn't even know how to fire a revolver. Hanna killed his man."

"Not so loud: you never know who may be passing."

"You make me tired. And I've got a headache: I always get a headache when I go to the cinema during the day. What shall we do now? Stand here and discuss the weather like English tourists?"

"Are you hungry?"

"No."

"You must eat. That's why you have a headache."

"I'm not hungry."

"You must have a meal before you go to Chapelle. It's five thirty now, so we'll have to hurry if you're to be at the Hôtel de l'Univers et de la Chapelle by seven. We'll go back to the Saint-André and get the cunt—if you'll forgive the expression —to make us a meal."

"All right. But first you must excuse me: there's something in this window that I've wanted for a long time and I've just realized that I can no longer resist it."

"Well, be quick."

Nefissa went into the shop: a perfumer's. Salah saw the assistant take a beribboned bottle from the summit of a display in the center of the window: the assistant packed the bottle in a carton and wrapped it in gay paper: he saw Nefissa pay for it with two hundred-franc notes: there seemed to be very little change. Nefissa was smiling when she left the shop.

The Café-Tabac Saint-André-des-Arts now held more customers, most of them spinning out the endless Left Bank afternoon to its conclusion over a cup of coffee or a glass of wine. Two dour-faced young men were drinking beer and keeping time with their feet to the jukebox, which was playing a martial air, "Tiens! voilà du boudin": the marching song of the Foreign Legion. They might have been German tourists. The manager went into the kitchen when the two Algerians entered the café.

"What's the matter with the cunt?" Salah asked. "I beg your pardon, mademoiselle."

"I hope he hasn't dropped the boat."

"Perhaps he's afraid you'll stick a thorn into him," Salah said.

He said nothing more for several minutes while they waited to be served; but no one came, not even the white-coated waiter.

"What are you dreaming about?" Nefissa asked.

"I was thinking how nice it would be to be able to shoot like the sheriff."

"Haven't you got a gun?"

"No. I used to have a gun, but I was more at home with a knife. Nowadays I don't carry either, because the police often pick me up and I'm supposed to be a harmless Algerian pimp selling postcards and making money out of one or two girls. I'm not even a *caïd* any more. Just a pimp. It is the role which the Organization has assigned me."

"I wonder what Hanna is doing?"

"I wonder if they'll give me a fighting job before the war

ends. But the war is nearly over. They say there are going to
be more talks at Evian. De Gaulle won't let the war go on:
the French people are sick of it. It's only the OAS fanatics
who are trying to keep it alive."

"Politics bores me."

"Then why are you fighting?"

"To free my people: because I can tell right from wrong.
But I don't want to talk about it any more. That was all right
when I was fifteen, but now I'm twenty-one I've heard the war
discussed from every possible angle and it bores me."

"What will you do when it's over?"

"I'll be a woman."

"You're a woman already."

"No, I'm a militant. But I've promised myself that I shall be
a woman before I die."

"I suppose I'll go on selling postcards as I've always done,"
Salah said.

The martial strains of "Le Boudin" faded and Nefissa stood
up.

"Excuse me," she said. "I've heard enough colonialist
music and there's something I must do."

She went over to the jukebox, passing the dour-faced young
men on the way: they were curiously alike: cropped hair and
thick lips. Each wore a parachute badge in his buttonhole.
They stared at Nefissa with the curiosity of young bulls.

Nefissa marched across to the cashier, a woman all beady
and black, and changed one of the shining NF 5 pieces for ten
of the old dull-nickel fifty-franc pieces. She selected one
record: "Jamais le dimanche," and then shot the remaining
nine coins into the slot and seemed to select the buttons at
random; she went downstairs to the lavatory as Melina
Mercouri began to sing to the music of a bouzouki.

She went through the swing doors below, but not into the
lavatory that served both sexes. She stood before the mirror,
put her bag on the table, and unwrapped the parcel she had
bought in the Boul' Mich'. It was a bottle of Balenciaga's Le
Dix. She pressed it once to herself and then unbuttoned her

leather coat and loosened the tie belt. She took the stopper out of the bottle and inhaled deeply with either nostril. Then she put back her head and poured the contents between her breasts and inclined her head and poured the rest down the nape of her neck until she felt it trickle between her buttocks. She inhaled the aroma that was now her own and dropped the bottle into the wastebasket.

It was then that she looked in the mirror and saw a man rummaging in her bag.

She turned and the man withdrew his hand, holding a pistol: it was one of the dour-faced men from above.

"What are you doing?" she asked him.

"Taking away your pistol," he told her.

"You daren't use it," Nefissa said.

"No," he said. "But I could use this and I will if I must." He spoke guttural French: Teutonic French.

He had dropped the automatic into his jacket pocket and, in the same motion, produced a switchblade. He held it in his left hand as though it had grown from his fingers.

"Quite a *blouson noir*," Nefissa said.

"You smell like an Algiers bordel," he said.

"You should know," Nefissa told him.

The thick lips made a grimace.

"Let's go," he said. "My friend is waiting with your friend."

He motioned with the switchblade and Nefissa turned toward the stairs. He stepped beside her, moving like a bantamweight though built like a heavyweight, and encircled her waist with the hand that held the switchblade. The blade now pricked Nefissa just below the ribs.

"You are familiar, m'sieu, and we haven't been introduced," Nefissa said.

The dour-faced man said nothing but pricked her diaphragm with the knife so that they mounted the stairs, he with the armed hand concealed in the folds of her coat, and she moving quite impartially, as though protected by her perfume, in an aura like a first-remembered spring.

They went through the café, and past the song of Mercouri,

to the terrace where Salah awaited them, escorted by the other dour-faced man, and turning upon Nefissa the eyes of a spaniel surprised in a larder.

Then the four of them went in two couples, the two men leading, down the place Saint-Michel and across the quai des Grands-Augustins and down the steps to the lower embankment beside the Seine.

Nefissa stopped halfway down the steps, wincing.

"What's the matter?"

"I can't go on with your knife sticking into me."

The man lowered the point of his knife so that it was no longer in contact with her flesh; then she fought. She caught the man's right hand, which held the knife within the folds of her coat, forcing it up and away, and tripped him with her right foot; she went forward and bent her back so that the bulk of him went up and over her narrow shoulders and he went down the steps, the knife clattering before him, the man rolling from step to step, arms outflung, his unprotected head cannoning off the stonework, and Nefissa's bag, which had been over her left arm, tumbling its little vanities in his trail.

Nefissa turned and ran up the steps.

The first of the dour-faced men heard the scuffle and turned; Salah strained away from the knife; the man killed Salah by thrusting up beneath the ribs and pressing the frail body down on the blade; Salah died so quickly that he made no noise before falling down the steps as the man withdrew the knife. The dirty postcards spilled out of Salah's pockets and spread themselves about his body like a discarded hand.

Nefissa was nearing the top of the steps when she saw a young man hurrying down. He was an elegant young man with an austere profile beneath a Tyrolean hat and a yellow silk scarf knotted at the neck of his covert coat.

"Help!" Nefissa shouted. "Help!"

He came to her, taking the steps three at a time: he caught her right wrist and forced it up between her shoulderblades; he whipped off the yellow silk scarf and forced it into her

open mouth as she cried out. Then he forced her down the
steps to the embankment and pulled her into an archway that
concealed them from people crossing the pont Saint-Michel.

The dour-faced man who had killed Salah was bending
over the man Nefissa had tripped and thrown. This man was
sitting up and groaning; his head was bloody but his limbs
were functioning.

"Right," said the man who held Nefissa. "Let's get this over
quickly."

The man drew back his weapon for an underarm thrust;
the man in the hat checked him with a gesture of his free
hand. He might have been demonstrating some point of eti-
quette.

"Mark her," he said. "Don't kill her. She must live to show
what happened to her. That is how terrorism is spread."

The knife was already stained with Salah's blood. The dour-
faced man used it like a surgeon to make three incisions in
Nefissa's right cheek. While this was happening the man in the
hat spoke to Nefissa as though she were being paraded before
him as a defaulter, speaking French with the combination of
precision and volubility that marks an educated Frenchman
expounding his favorite theme.

"You mustn't think that you Algerian terrorists can get
away with your dirty games in France any longer, my dear. If
the police can't deal with you the OAS will. You're lucky, my
dear, because you might have killed one of my men and we
should have had to execute you for that. But we'll let you
go as a warning to your friends. Keep away from the Saint-
André: it's under our protection now and the OAS always
gives value for money. When the traitors have been turned
out of the Elysée Palace it is we who will rule. And when that
day comes you can dismiss your childish notions of an Algerian Algeria; Algeria is as French as the ground beneath our
feet."

The man with the switchblade stood back and gestured at
Nefissa's face.

"There you are, captain. They couldn't have done a neater job at the Hôpital de l'Hôtel-Dieu."

"Don't gloat," the captain told him. "It's an act of war, not a work of art. Is that fool fit to walk?"

The man Nefissa had tripped and thrown had been sitting on the steps and trying to stanch the blood flowing from his nose with a handkerchief. He stood up and made a rudimentary attempt to stand at attention.

"*Ja, Herr Kapitan.*"

"Then you can go, my dear. There's nothing wrong with you that a few months' plastic surgery can't put right, and I'm sure an organization as wealthy as the FLN can find the money for the operations. And if they can't, I don't doubt that plenty of our half-baked intellectuals and liberals will stand treat in return for the publicity. Off you go."

He stuffed the scarf deeper into her mouth, gave her a pat on the behind, and pushed her up the steps.

She began to run and to tear the scarf from her mouth as she ran; when she got it free she began to scream; she went on screaming and suddenly there were two Municipal policemen standing at the top of the steps.

Nefissa got between them and turned to the scene below.

Salah's body lay on the embankment, but they had turned him over so that he might have been a sleeping tramp. The captain and the man who had marked Nefissa were having difficulty keeping the injured man on his feet; he appeared to be complaining of internal pain.

"Murderers!" Nefissa shouted, pointing down at them. "Murderers!"

The guardians of the peace looked at each other and drew their MAS 35 automatic pistols.

The captain raised his hand and pointed at Nefissa:

"Arrest that girl."

The *flics* hesitated.

"He's a murderer," Nefissa shouted. "That's his gang down there and there's the body of the man they've murdered."

The *flics* looked at each other.

"Gentlemen," the captain said, his voice wearing authority like a uniform, "as a French officer I order you to arrest that Algerian, that terrorist."

The *flics* turned to lay hands on Nefissa.

But Nefissa was halfway across the road, dodging her way amid a fury of horn-blowing. The *flics* followed, more decorously, gaining right of way by the authority of an up-raised arm or blast on a whistle. Nefissa was running toward the place Saint-André-des-Arts: the two *flics* reached the pavement and began to run after her; people were already stopping to gape. Another *flic* on the eastern side of the place Saint-Michel began running parallel to them.

She went down into the Metro in the place Saint-André-des-Arts; the two *flics* followed; the third doubled back to the Saint-Michel entrance.

It was almost six o'clock: the rush hour had begun. Nefissa sped between the scurrying office girls; the *flics* forced their way, encountering much obstruction and abuse despite their drawn pistols. Nefissa plunged her right hand into the ticket pocket of her leather coat, found a ticket book, tore off a ticket and thrust it before the woman at the barrier, and then ran into the elevator, scarf pressed to her bleeding cheek. The *flic* who had come by Saint-Michel saw her as the elevator doors shut, but was delayed by having to force his way through the barrier; he warned his colleagues, sent one of them to telephone to the next station, Odéon, one to guard the elevator in case Nefissa came back that way, and ran for the stairs to the platform. He saw but could not stop Nefissa getting into an incoming train by literally throwing herself into the solid wall of bodies; the doors closed behind her. The *flic* blew his whistle as the train moved off and the guard waved and shrugged his shoulders.

The train was traveling southwest: at Odéon there were two *flics* waiting to board the train, but they could not decide which of the five cars to enter and Nefissa slipped by them in the outgoing crowd. Instead of going out by the exit she cut through connecting tunnels to the opposite platform. Instead of waiting on the platform itself she loitered by the automatic door, slipping through as it began to close, and boarded a train marked *"Direction Clignancourt."* The train was less crowded and she was able to press into the interior and hang on to a strap while she studied the line map. The next stop was Saint-Michel: to get off there was unthinkable; after that Cité, which would place her on an island which contained the Prefecture of Police. The first place she could hope to get off was Châtelet, on the Right Bank, and trust the police were not yet guarding all the stations on the route.

They went through Saint-Michel and the Cité without incident. The train was swaying violently as it always did on this section of the line. A short woman, standing beside Nefissa, dabbed at her neck and screeched:

"Shit! It's blood."

"I'm sorry," Nefissa said.

"You're wounded, girl. I thought you had a bad cold."

"It's nothing," Nefissa said. "Just a scratch."

"You're bleeding like a pig. Let me see."

Before Nefissa, who was straphanging with one hand and holding the scarf to her face with the other, could resist, the little woman had bared her cheek. She stared at it for a moment: the flesh was white from Nefissa's pressure; the wound stood out like a symbol.

"Your cheek. Look at your cheek. Look at her cheek. Have you seen her cheek?"

Nefissa tried to see her reflection in the windows; but the train was pulling into Châtelet, so she raised the scarf again and pushed past the little woman, past the interrogative eyes of the other passengers, and lost herself in the crowd getting off. There were no police guarding the exit.

Still keeping in the crowds she crossed the rue Saint-Honoré and then plunged into the maze of streets about Les Halles, where the pavements were still slippery with the morning's deliveries. She turned a corner and stopped, looking instinctively for the vanity mirror in her bag; but she had left her bag on the embankment. She walked on faster than before, the blood pumping in her cheek until the scarf was sodden and the sight of the blood made her stop and puke. A big market porter came up to her to offer assistance; she turned away; he followed her shouting that there was a pharmacy across the street. She looked up and saw the green cross outlined in neon tubing. The big porter was still shouting advice and beginning to attract attention. She went into the pharmacy and the porter went away satisfied.

There was only a young man in a white smock in the shop. Nefissa asked for some adhesive tape; the pharmacist suggested that she sit down; Nefissa's knees seemed to liquefy as she took a chair.

"What happened, mademoiselle?" the pharmacist asked.

"I work at the cash register in a butcher's shop," she told him. "I slipped and fell against a meathook. I'm afraid . . . afraid that I may be disfigured."

"Wait a moment, mademoiselle. I'll clean and dress the wound for you, but then you'd better go to a hospital."

The pharmacist came back with a roll of adhesive tape, gauze swabs, and a bottle of iodine. Nefissa disclosed her cheek. The pharmacist seemed to become even younger and even more conscientious; he stared at the wound for several seconds but said nothing. He daubed the wound with iodine until Nefissa winced. He threw the soiled swab into a bin and gave Nefissa a second swab to hold to her cheek.

"Now I must go and telephone for an ambulance," he told her.

"I don't want to go to a hospital," she said. "I just want some adhesive tape for my face until I get home."

"But you must go to a hospital for treatment at once. Otherwise you may be disfigured for life. It is a matter outside my competence. You'll need cosmetic surgery."

"Never mind that. Give me the adhesive tape."

"The police must be informed."

"Why the police? What has an accident like this to do with the police? My employers will look after the insurance."

"Have you seen the wound, mademoiselle?"

"No," Nefissa said. "I've seen nothing."

She was crying.

The pharmacist walked over to the wall and took down a mirror displayed for sale; he gave Nefissa the iodine bottle so that he could hold the mirror with both hands for her to see herself full-face.

The mirror showed Nefissa that her right cheek had been deeply incised with the sign of a cross within a circle.

"Whoever wielded the meathook was an expert," the pharmacist said. "But I don't think it could have been done with a meathook."

"What does that matter to you?"

"To me personally it does not matter. But to me professionally it matters a great deal. A wound has been inflicted upon you, mademoiselle."

"Do you think I don't know that?"

"And such a wound. A distinctive wound. I have seen photographs of such wounds inflicted on prisoners at Bizerte. It is a wound that forms the insignia of the OAS. Someone has set his signature upon your face."

"Oh, get on with the treatment."

"There is nothing more I can do but telephone the police. It is the duty of a pharmacist to inform the police of all malicious woundings that are brought to his attention. There is a war on, mademoiselle."

"I had noticed it. Why can't you just forget that you've ever seen me?"

"Partly because I must ensure that you have proper treatment and partly because it's my duty. Supposing that you were picked up by the police in the next street and they asked you where you'd been treated? You tell them that you've been here and they come to ask why I've concealed it. My employer gets to hear of it and fires me. I'm only an assistant here; my employer is in a bistro down the street; I'm expected to cover up for him because he drinks. Consequently I must do my duty as a pharmacist. I can take no chances."

"Neither can I," Nefissa said.

She pulled the stopper from the iodine bottle and jerked the contents into the pharmacist's face. He screamed and dropped the mirror to clap his hands over his eyes: Nefissa recovered the adhesive tape from among the fragments and ran: the pharmacist was still screaming.

She found sanctuary in Notre-Dame de Bonne Nouvelle: in the incense-perfumed gloom she was able, by bending over a stoup of holy water to find her reflection, to cover the wound with adhesive. She sponged the blood from her coat with water from the font; the church was quite deserted. She looked at her wrist watch by the light of the candles at the Lady altar: it was twenty-five past six. She went out.

In the street she found a taxi and asked him to drive direct to the Hôtel de l'Univers et de la Chapelle, rue Fleury, in the eighteenth *arrondissement*. Then she recollected.

"I've lost my bag," she told the driver. "Will you trust me if I give you my name and address? You can have the money tomorrow."

"Mademoiselle," the taxi driver said, "I am a Frenchman. I never trust Algerians. Fuck off."

So she walked to the Metro at Strasbourg-Saint-Denis and used the last ticket of her book to get to La Chapelle. At this point the Metro emerged from the earth and ran overhead for the length of the boulevard de la Chapelle. She could see down into it from the station, see people talking in groups and hurrying down the street, but she could not see so far as the rue Fleury.

While she was looking through the fencing, two men came up behind Nefissa and pinioned her arms. They had the somber elegance of successful businessmen: the one on the left was young, shockheaded, thickly mustached; the man on the right was of prime age, black hair in a crew cut, thick-faced, scorbutic.

"Mademoiselle Nefissa Saddok, I charge you with conspiring to murder Auxiliary Guardian Mohammed Kacemi this morning," the man on the right said.

"How did you find me?"

"Easy. You left your handbag on the quai des Grands-Augustins and we found your identity papers in it. The OAS tipped off the Metropolitan Police about how they'd carved you up. Then the case came to us. We knew you'd gone into the Metro and we guessed you wouldn't be able to take a taxi because we found money in your bag."

"So you got those OAS cunts?"

"Unfortunately, no. They got away while the police were chasing you, but they gave the tip by telephone."

"And if your grandmother had had testicles, inspector—you are an inspector, aren't you?—she would have been your grandmother."

"Not all the Municipal Police share our antipathy toward the OAS: some even regard them as allies against North Africans like yourself."

"So I'm in the hands of the *barbouzes*."

"Don't be so melodramatic, my dear. I find shaving lotion sufficient for my vanity and I would never dream of disguising myself with a beard, let alone a false one. To be precise, you are in the hands of the Direction et Surveillance du Territoire."

"I'm honored. I was afraid that I might be arrested by a common *flic*."

"We've been interested in you for a long time, my dear. You've been making too many converts among the intellectuals."

"That doesn't explain how you've come to connect me with the death of Kacemi."

"The police found the gun that killed Kacemi in a parcel addressed to you at the Hôtel de l'Univers et de la Chapelle."

"I suppose *flics* always intercept the mail?"

"Not at all. The parcel, as you well know, was in the mailbox at the hotel. Kacemi fired back before he died. He missed his assassin and killed two innocent bystanders; but he was a good shot although he was dying: he was aiming at the door of the hotel because he knew where the shots had come from, and two of his bullets hit the mailbox through which he'd been shot and tore open the parcel that his assassin had left there after putting the pistol inside it."

"What has happened to Hanna?"

"They killed him nearly an hour ago."

"Bastards."

"They had no alternative. He put up quite a fight. He killed two of our people—one of them was a French sergeant—and wounded another quite badly . . . got him in the chest: he may not live. Don't pity Hanna. He was just another gunman."

"He was just a poet and I loved him. Do what you like to me: I don't want to go on living."

"That's just little-girl talk," the inspector said. "You'll get over it."

The man on the left handcuffed Nefissa with her hands behind her back; the inspector took off his own gloves and pulled them high up her wrists so that the handcuffs could not be seen. She tried to kick his shins, but he stamped on her feet and brought tears to her eyes.

"That's for your own good," he explained. "There have been enough incidents for one day and there are people about who might be so foolish as to try and rescue you. Discourage the idea: we have wider powers than the police and we don't hesitate to use them. Besides, think of your own people: any more shooting and the *harkis* will undoubtedly begin a *ratissage*. And don't try any more of that crude stuff that worked with the OAS. Understand? Let's go."

So they went down the wide wooden steps to the street where a black Peugeot 403 without police markings awaited them. There were two other men in plain clothes in the front seats; while Nefissa was seated in the back between her captors, the man beside the driver bent over a radio transmitter and reported her arrest to the chief of intervention police for the eighteenth *arrondissement*.

"Are you taking me to the interrogation center at Vincennes or to the rue des Saussaies?" Nefissa asked.

"Why, to the rue des Saussaies, of course," the inspector told her. "You don't think we'd treat you as a mere suspect, do you? You don't need to be sorted out. You've done far too well for that."

"So I'm not to be brought to trial?"

"We'll see," the inspector promised. "If you're a good girl we may even allow you to stand trial."

"And otherwise?"

"We'll see. This is war."

"Thank you for reminding me."

The car had now left behind the drabness of northern Paris and was entering the tourist-bedecked place Clichy. The driver entered the rue de Leningrad which led into the rue d'Astorg and followed it through the place des Saussaies and into the rue des Saussaies. They were now in the heart of the fashionable eighth *arrondissement*, just behind the Elysée Palace. The car stopped before an impartial grey façade where a man in a noncommittal blue uniform opened double doors and waved them into an inner courtyard.

They took Nefissa out of the car and across the courtyard and through a door into a passage floored with marble that led into a small room that might once have been a powder closet.

"Right," the inspector said. "You can cool off here. Are you armed?"

"No," she said.

"Find out," the inspector told the detective.

The young man with the mustache searched Nefissa with clinical thoroughness and without familiarity, as a doctor might examine a patient; he avoided her kicks, but she succeeded in spitting in his face.

"You never give up, do you?" the young man said.

"No," she said. "Do you?"

"I don't think so," he told her. "I was once in the position that you are in, when I was taken by the Viets in Indochina."

"Stop being subverted by her," the inspector said. "You can take off the handcuffs now."

The young man unlocked the gyves from Nefissa's wrists and moved out of range. Nefissa sat heavily on the only chair in the room. She massaged her wrists and looked at them from beneath the beetling shock of hair.

"What are you going to do to me?" she asked.

"Nothing," the inspector said. "We're going to give you time to reflect. You and your friend Hanna have left us hungry. We're going to have dinner."

They went out and locked the double door. Nefissa got up and then sat down again. Her mouth was magenta. She began to pant. She began to massage her wrists again, but the movement of her right arm made her wince. Presently she lay back in the chair and pressed her right hand between her breasts.

Nefissa was like this when six men came into the room: one was a uniformed major of the Municipal Police wearing steel-rimmed spectacles; two were *flics*; two were *harkis*; the sixth man wore no uniform, but deferred to those who did.

"She's our prisoner now," the major said. "We'll take her downstairs."

"Of course, sir," the man in plain clothes said.

He was the first to leave the room.

"I remember you," Nefissa told the major, "from the seventeenth of October. You searched me."

"Take her away," the major said.

Nefissa got to her feet and struck out when they came to her; her face was convulsed. The two *harkis* evaded her blows and picked her up; they carried her out into the hall and to the stairs leading down into the basement. At the head of the stairs they let her go; Nefissa went over and over down the steps, making only feeble efforts to break her fall. The police followed her and the two *harkis* picked her up at the bottom of the steps. She was whimpering in her pain, but not crying out.

"Stop that," the major shouted. "We're going to do this the clean way."

"That was for Kacemi," one of the *harkis* said.

"Shut up," the major said. "I'm saving her for *la question.*

Jesus Christ, look at the mess you've made of her already."

The Celtic cross that the OAS had carved on Nefissa's right cheek had reopened; one of her eyebrows was split; blood was streaming from both nostrils.

Nefissa looked up at them.

"Cunts," she said.

She spat blood at them.

The major stepped back and fastidiously wiped some specks from his trousers.

"Help her up," he ordered. "Let's see if anything's broken."

The *harkis* got Nefissa to her feet and found that she could stand, though swaying.

"Good," the major said. "Very good. Let's go. And take care of her. I'm saving her for something special."

They took her into a basement room. It was barely furnished: a table two meters square, rather stained, with leather straps at each corner; a bath with a clothes rack suspended from a pulley above it; what looked like a army field telephone with terminals; what looked like a pair of compasses with a wire running to a wall socket; and a few hard chairs.

There was a curious odor about the place, like the memory of a bad illness; Nefissa's new fragrance cut clear across it.

"Sit her down," the major ordered the *harkis*. "But hold her."

The major himself took a chair and set it down about two yards from Nefissa. He straddled it so that he looked at her over the back. Then he took off his spectacles and began to polish them with a piece of chamois leather.

"We're going to make you talk," the major told her.

"No," she said. "You're going to put me to *la question*."

"Torture will make you talk."

"We have so little in common; I can't think what we'd find to talk about."

"Don't try to be funny. You'll talk."

"Nothing you can do to me will make me talk."

"Have you seen what is in this room?"

"I know all about the water and electrical treatments."

"That is only the beginning. That is clean torture."

"And then?" she asked.

Her eyes had become so enormous within their dark rings that they seemed to fill her face. They were filled with tawny light. The disfigured face was forgotten. She was quite calm. All five men, even the two *harkis* who held her down, were conscious of the eyes; it was as though they were standing on the brink of erupting pools of lava; the major lost the thread of his discourse. He put his glasses on again with only one lens polished, as though to shield himself from her gaze.

"What will you do to me when the water and electrical treatments have failed?" Nefissa prompted him.

"We'll make a *cassoulet*," the major said. He smiled slightly and looked at the two *flics*. They sniggered. "And you, my dear, will be the meat."

"You mean that you'll line the bath with broken bottles and strap me into it," Nefissa said. "I know about that."

"You're very well informed," the major told her.

"You daren't do that to me," Nefissa said. "You might get away with the water and electrical treatments because I suppose the courts would cover up for you, even though there are still some members of the Paris bar who will defend us. But you'd never get away with a *cassoulet* because my father is a senior member of the French administration in Algiers and would demand my body."

"We know all about your father," the major said. "We know he is loyal and influential, and what is even more important for a Mussulman, he has money. But he will suspect nothing—at least he will be able to prove nothing. The mark on your cheek is as good as a guarantee that all that was done to you has been done by the OAS. The police will, of course, rescue you from the OAS, but it may be too late."

"It makes no difference," Nefissa said. "I'll die before I talk."

"They all say that at first."

"I know it."

The major looked at her and then looked away and took

off his spectacles and began to polish the lens he had already polished.

"Well, get on with it," he shouted at the two *harkis*. "Strip her."

The senior of the two Parisian policemen, a corporal, walked over to the major and stood to attention.

"Permission to get some wine, sir?"

The two *harkis* had begun their work, but Nefissa was lashing out with her feet. She got one on the shin, and the second drew back his fist.

"Don't hit her, you fool," the major shouted. "I don't want her spoiled. Be gentle or I'll blow your navels through your assholes. Treat her gently: treat her like a bride. Stupid buggers. Put the cuffs back if you can't control her. Get out of the way, corporal. I want to watch. What do you want? Wine? Barbarian. Get some whisky. Real English whisky. The stuff in dented bottles. Get two bottles. Take this. Get three bottles. Tonight we'll drink like policemen."

He gave the corporal a note for one hundred New Francs and another for fifty and waved him aside. Two spots of red below the cheekbones illuminated his otherwise colorless face.

The corporal moved closer to the major and lowered his voice:

"Shall I get some beer for these animals? They're not used to spirits. There's no telling what they might do. They're overexcited already."

"All right, buy some beer. It's all on expenses. Mongénéral is host tonight . . . No, let them share the whisky. I'm going to make them into real *flics*."

"Yes, sir."

The right eyelid of the corporal flickered as he looked at his colleague. The guardian of the peace took a chair beside the major to watch the two *harkis* with Nefissa.

They had unfastened the leather skirt at the waist and drawn it down about her ankles to prevent her kicking; but the upper garments defied them because her wrists were still shackled and her leather coat would not split at the seams.

"You'll have to take the handcuffs off again," the major told them. "I told you I don't want her harmed until she's on the table."

"She'll fight if we release her hands," one of the *harkis* said.

"So what? Can't the two of you undress a girl? What sort of auxiliaries are you? What did they teach you at police school?"

"They taught us to strike," the second *harki* said.

"I'll teach you when not to strike," the major told them. "Learn to combine the twin arts—violence and restraint— and you have the secret of ultimate power."

Nefissa spat blood at him.

"The secret of power is freedom," she said. "The exercise of power inhibits the master as much as the slave: both are prisoners of the same system and are governed by the same rules."

"You've taken part in too many debates at the Sorbonne," the major told her. "There is all the difference in the world between principle and practice. Can you honestly tell me that you wouldn't rather be me at this moment? And yet the same exercises in power have brought us to this confrontation. Only yours has failed."

"I would rather be myself than you under any circumstances," she said. "You also forget that the balance of power changes."

One of the *harkis* had unlocked the handcuffs; Nefissa jabbed her right elbow backward and upward and caught the man with the keys under the chin, making him bite his tongue; his colleague twisted her arm and she set her teeth in his hand; the first *harki* swung the keys at her face.

"Stop that," the major ordered.

"The cow," the first *harki* said. "The treacherous cow."

"I said I didn't want her spoiled. Is that all they taught you at police school? Can't the two of you undress her without violence? You've got to prove yourself good *flics* tonight. One of you pinion her arms while the other takes her shoes off for a start. Then if she kicks it won't matter. Then get a damp cloth and wipe her face. I can't see the expression for the blood."

The guardian of the peace was leaning back in his chair, helpless with laughter.

"You know, major," he gurgled, "this is better than the Grand Guignol."

"Cowards," Nefissa shouted.

"That's better," the major said. "Now we're beginning to get some reaction. I love to hear them talk."

"Give me something to drink if you want to hear me talk," Nefissa said. "Give me some water."

"Get her a glass of water," the major ordered. "Didn't you hear what the lady asked for?"

The *harki* with the keys took a cup from a shelf above the bath and ran it beneath the tap.

"May I piss in it, sir?"

"No, animal, give her the water. We're going to be scientific, you understand. She's a militant, an intellectual, and she must be treated as she deserves."

Nefissa drank half the water and spat the second mouthful into the *harki*'s face.

"She's making a fool of us," the man with the bitten hand said.

The guardian of the peace was almost prostrate with laughter.

"No," the major contradicted him. "She's making a fool of herself. She's betraying herself into behaving like a beast. She's supposed to be good at converting people to the FLN, but she hasn't tried it on you two, has she? The French culture is only a veneer. Now you can see the sort of people we're fighting against."

"I'm fighting you with your own weapons," Nefissa said.

"I've served in Algeria," the major told her. "I've seen what your *fellaghas* do to French women and children. That wasn't scientific. You're savages, animals, fig-tree trunks. The more we educate you the more treacherous you become. Tonight I'm going to prove it."

"Major," the *harki* with the bitten hand said, "with respect I must protest. We also are Algerians and we are loyal French citizens."

"You still have a long way to go before you become Frenchmen," the major told them. "To begin with you can learn how to undress a woman without violence."

By the time the corporal had returned with the whisky Nefissa was stripped. She had an interesting body: fawn and downy as that of a deer; the legs much longer than the trunk and shapely to the knee but slender in the thigh; breasts mottled like pears beneath a concave chest. The high notch between her thighs was unconcealed by pubic hair.

The bitten *harki* prodded her uterus.

"That's a fine thing for a young girl," he told her. "You've shaved yourself like a matron."

"I was waiting for Hanna," she said. "I had hoped to be with him tonight."

"We can promise you more excitement if less pleasure," the major said. "Corporal, open that bottle. We're going to need it."

The corporal opened the bottle and passed it to the major, who drank a little and passed it back to him. The corporal drank well and passed it to the guardian of the peace, who drank and coughed and drank again before offering it to the *harkis*.

"We can't drink," the *harki* with the bitten hand said. The hand was bleeding freely: Nefissa had small, pointed teeth. "There's no telling what this cow might do."

"What's become of *la furie française?*" Nefissa asked. "You say you're Frenchmen, don't you? Don't you want to behave like Frenchmen?"

"She's making a fool of us," the other *harki* said.

"Put her in the bath," the major said. "Cool her off. Then come and have a drink. See if the whisky will grow you ballocks enough to deal with a woman."

"She isn't in bed," the *harki* with the bitten hand protested.

"You know your trouble?" the major asked him. "You have no sense of humor. Fill the bath and put her in it."

The *harkis* lifted Nefissa out of her chair and held her while the guardian of the peace lowered the pulleys of the clothes rack, and then they trussed her to it by wrists and ankles, as a chef might truss a chicken over a spit. They used elastic ropes with metal clips of the kind used to secure luggage on the roof rack of a family car; by the time they had done the bath was filled with cold water, and then the guardian of the peace lowered Nefissa into it until she was submerged, all save mouth and nostrils.

Then the *harkis* had a drink of whisky and passed it back to the major. The major drank a little more and passed it back to the corporal, who drank a great deal and passed it to the guardian of the peace, who drank even more and passed it to the *harkis*, who tried to drink as much as he—and failed.

Then the bottle went on its third round and the major passed around his cigarettes, which were Boyards, and the guardian of the peace lit them, and the bottle began its fourth round.

Everyone was swaying now, sitting or standing, except for the major.

"Have you ever read 'Eminkvay?" the major asked them.

"No," the corporal said. The guardian of the peace smiled and the *harkis* shook their heads.

"I've read him in the American," the major told them.

"That's a great gift," the guardian of the peace said, "to be able to read American."

"Have you ever read Vailland?" the major asked.

The guardian of the peace got to his feet:

"He's a French author, isn't he?"

"That's right."

"I don't have time to read much except *L'Aurore*," the guardian of the peace confessed. "And *L'Equipe* when the Tour de France is on."

"You should read 'Eminkvay or Vailland," the major said.

"Yes, of course, sir."

"Empty that bottle."

The guardian of the peace did so before speaking:

"Excuse me, major, but I think the prisoner is drowning. The tap drips."

"Well, get her out. I told you I didn't want her spoiled."

They lifted Nefissa out of the bath: she was vomiting water.

"Let's fill her up again with the hose and jump on her," the *harki* with the bitten hand suggested.

"Animals," the major said. "Put her on the table."

The *harkis* took great time and trouble in getting Nefissa onto the table and strapping her down; they swayed a good deal and lacked synchronization; they dropped her once; she shivered all the time but made no protest. Her body was all livid-to-blue and goose-pimpled; her belly was swelled fish-white; her face had stopped bleeding and the wounds and bruises were vivid in the sodden flesh.

"Open another bottle," the major ordered.

He moved his chair to the foot of the table, from which position he had an uninterrupted view between Nefissa's thighs.

The guardian of the peace opened the second bottle of Dimple Haig and gulped from the neck. The major reproved him.

"Give her some."

"That cow?"

"That's an order."

The guardian of the peace tilted some of the spirit between Nefissa's blue lips; it was like a reincarnation: she began to swear.

The major stood up holding the empty bottle and leaned over Nefissa: he prodded her vagina with the neck of the bottle.

"Do you know what I'm going to do?"

"I know what you're going to try," she said. "It's too late."

"Hanna?"

"No. I wish it had been. There are no virgins in the revolution. Virginity is a medical illusion and a moral myth."

The major shattered the bottle against the wall.

"She may be lying," the bitten *harki* suggested. "We could empty the second bottle and try it."

"These bottles are the wrong shape anyway," the guardian of the peace said. "The neck is too short. A wine bottle is better."

"A Kronenbourg bottle is better," the corporal contradicted. He had the whisky now. "The neck is long and swells at the base."

"A goose-necked bottle is best of all," the guardian of the peace asserted. "Like rosé d'Anjou. It goes all the way in to the top of the womb. That makes them squirm. If it doesn't work in one hole you can always try it in the other."

The corporal scowled at him over the whisky and the guardian of the peace smiled back.

"I've had experience," he said and touched his left breast. The ribbons displayed there showed that he had served in Madagascar and Algeria: he had been awarded the Croix de guerre. The corporal wore no ribbons.

"Get on with the electrical treatment," the major ordered.

He restraddled the chair and took the whisky bottle from the corporal. He drank more deeply than before. He passed the bottle to the *harkis*.

"You two can take it easy now," he told them. "You can see how the job should be done."

The major took off his spectacles and began to polish them as the corporal and the guardian of the peace got to work; he was like a myopic child about to witness a party treat.

"Which shall we begin with?" the corporal asked. "The *tire-boulette* or the *gégène*?"

"Both. I think this is a case for shock treatment."

"Certainly, sir."

The guardian of the peace pushed one of the terminals of the field telephone up Nefissa's vagina and the other up her anus; the corporal arranged the points of the compass to align with her nipples.

"So this is the final flowering of French culture," Nefissa said.

It was as though she were speaking to them by long-distance telephone. The corporal looked at the major.

"Go ahead."

The guardian of peace began to turn the handle of the *gégène* and the corporal switched on the *tire-boulette*. The first shocks convulsed her: she was all goose pimples; then she was all sweat beads.

"Mother," Nefissa said. "Mother, mother, mother, mother . . ."

Then she was convulsed again. Then she was silent. She stopped moving. The sweat dried into great salt patches. She began to urinate helplessly and to excrete.

The corporal lifted the compass points.

"Shall we go on?" he asked. "I think she's passed out."

"Go on," the major said and passed the whisky to the *harkis*. He was looking over the top of his spectacles.

The *harkis* were the first to be sick, but they got to the bath; the guardian of the peace was sick over Nefissa's belly; the corporal put aside the compasses and sat down.

"She's done for," he said.

"Go on," the major said.

"I can't."

The corporal was sick between his feet.

The major got to his feet and went to an internal telephone set in the wall.

"Send down a doctor," he ordered. "One of the prisoners is ill."

The major drank some whisky by himself, and presently the inspector who had arrested Nefissa came into the room followed by a man with an empurpled face who carried a black Gladstone bag.

"What's all this?" asked the inspector.

He walked over to the table and released Nefissa's wrists; he took up her left wrist and then let it lie. The doctor took a stethoscope from the bag and began his examination.

"She passed out on us," the major said. "A most disappointing subject."

He offered the Dimple Haig to the inspector, who made a violent gesture of refusal.

"You're a disgrace to that uniform," the inspector told him.

"You forget yourself, inspector," the major said. He was livid and glinting.

"You're on DST territory now," the inspector said. "You may be my superior in rank, but I'm in charge of the case. What were you doing with my prisoner?"

"What you'd have done with her later."

"She was brought here for observation only. She was going to be turned over to the psychologists: we want to find out what goes to make that sort of militant rebel and we may be months finding another."

"What does it matter? You tell me, you security man. I'm just a policeman."

"We've got to find out why these people are resisting us so fanatically."

"It's a bit late for that now. The war will be settled over our heads by negotiation."

"The principle is the same. There will be other wars. All future wars will be wars of subversion unless there are nuclear wars. Subversion was once the last resort of the underprivileged, but it's become the most potent weapon in the world now that nuclear weapons have made formal warfare a form of suicide. And the only answer to subversion is conversion. That will be our job."

"You talk just as she did," the major said.

"What did she say when you tortured her?"

"Just cursed us and called for her mother."

The doctor came between them and began putting away his stethoscope.

"She didn't die by violence," the doctor said. "It was only a contributory cause. She had a weak heart. I can put that on the death certificate."

"I could have told you that," the inspector said. "We found a bottle of sal volatile in her bag and you could tell by the color of her lips."

"That confirms my diagnosis," the doctor said. "No doubt her own doctor would confirm the treatment. That looks like excellent Scotch whisky, major."

The inspector ignored the doctor and spoke to the major alone.

"What questions did you put to her?"

"None. First of all we had to get her into the mood to answer questions."

"What could she have told you?"

"You should know. You tell me you're in charge of the case."

"She could have told you nothing. Hanna is dead and so is her contact, the so-called Salah. She was just a militant, a good militant, but we know all about her contacts at the university: she had to work in the open to make converts, so the FLN could never entrust her with secret information. She had nothing to tell you and she knew it."

The major took off his spectacles and began to polish them; the doctor was sharing the second bottle of whisky with the *flics*; the inspector was snapping his fingers; the body of Nefissa, the rising fumes of her filth mingled with Le Dix, was forgotten; the argument continued.

"She was a subversive, wasn't she?" the major said. "You keep this room for questioning subversives, don't you?"

"Certainly, when they have something to reveal. You *flics* don't understand that: you're still fighting this war as though you were the Gestapo. We of the DST learned how to fight a modern war of subversion in Indochina."

The major replaced his spectacles and looked into the inspector's face.

"All that is beside the point," he said. "The girl must have had something to hide. Why else should she resist us?"